BDSM

THE LESBIAN COLLECTION

VICTORIA RUSH

COPYRIGHT

For the uninhibited...

TURN UP THE HEAT IN YOUR LIFE!

To receive more free books and other steamy stuff, sign up for my newsletter.

Victoria Rush Erotica

VOLUME ONE

THE DOMINATRIX

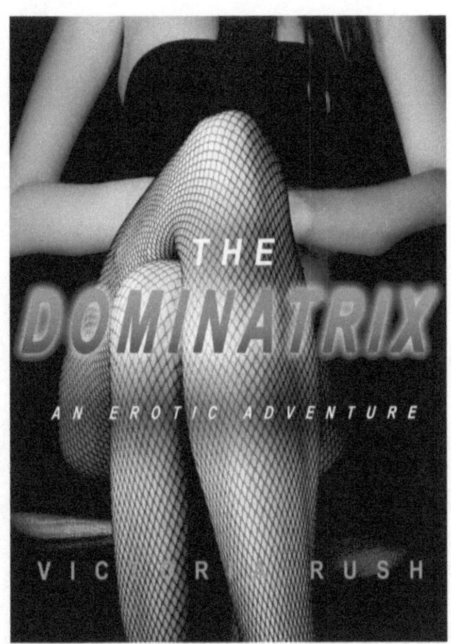

1

—————

BRAVE NEW WORLD

After my personal training sessions ended, I felt a new void in my sex life. Kate was incredibly hot and sexy and had pushed me past my limits in so many ways. She'd not only helped me restore my youthful body shape, she'd helped me realize that I could accomplish anything with the right motivation and workout plan.

But there was something else missing. I missed her guidance, her *commands*. There was something about the way she directed me through my paces that I found exhilarating and arousing. Even though she'd set me up with a self-directed routine to maintain my muscle tone, it wasn't nearly as much fun without her sexy body standing next to me, barking out orders to push out one more rep.

I needed a new life coach—one who'd push me beyond just my physical limits. I wanted a sex partner who'd fully take charge and *control* me. All I knew about BDSM was that it had something to do with bondage and domination. It was time to explore a new dimension to my sexuality.

I sat down in front of my computer and typed in the search box: *where to find a sexual master*. Near the top of the listings was a heading titled *Mistress Directory — Professional Mistresses and Dominatrix*

Contacts. I clicked on the link and a website popped up with a gallery of sexy women dressed in provocative leather outfits holding whips and chains. I scrolled through the images until I saw a sexy redhead named Mistress Velvet.

When I opened her page, my eyes widened as the screen toggled between a series of full-screen photographs of the redhead in various stages of undress. Each pose revealed more and more of her voluptuous figure. In the first slide, she lay on a white leather settee in a red push-up bra and garters. Her large natural breasts overflowed her top, with the edge of her pink nipples peeking over the seam. In the next slide, she lay facedown in a shiny black body suit with her legs playfully elevated. I stared at her tight round ass, fantasizing about burying my face in her deep sensuous cleft. The third panel showed her on her hands and knees in a corset and nylons, with her knees suggestively splayed over an assortment of sex toys. My pussy fluttered imagining her lowering herself over me.

Even more tantalizing than her centerfold-perfect figure was her incredible beauty. Her dark eyes peered at me under long eyelashes as her plump crimson lips pursed in a beckoning pout, her waist-length auburn hair cascading over every sensuous curve and valley of her magnificent figure. Whatever this vixen was selling, I wanted a piece of it. I clicked on her Profile tab where an introductory paragraph described her services:

Welcome to Velvet's Place. My name is Mistress Velvet, the supreme Sex Goddess and Dominatrix. My mission is to deliver the ultimate sensual experience and take you to new heights of pleasure through my unique style of sexual domination. I'm highly experienced with most fetishes and forms of BDSM. My specially-equipped pleasure chamber is equipped with state-of-the-art bondage furniture and stimulation equipment designed to tease and arouse you until you beg for mercy. Call now or click the chat box below for more information...

Bondage furniture? Stimulation equipment?
I had no idea what she had in mind, but I liked the idea of teasing

me until I begged for mercy. By the time I finished reading her profile, my panties were soaked all the way through imagining what it would be like to be her sex slave. I scanned toward the bottom of the page and clicked on the chat box, hoping somebody would be available at this late hour. My fingers hesitated over the keyboard, unsure how to initiate the discussion.

Is anyone there? I typed.

After a few seconds, three dots popped up in the reply window, indicating someone was responding on the other end.

Hello! someone named Velvet replied. *Welcome to Velvet's Place. How can we stimulate your senses today?*

Is this Mistress Velvet? I responded, hardly believing my luck getting hold of the proprietor on such short notice.

It is indeed. Although some people like to call me Goddess, Master, or Glaminatrix Velvet. I'm here to please. What's your kink?

What's my kink?! I thought, sitting back in surprise. *How do I respond to that kind of invitation?*

Well I'm kind of new to this whole thing, I typed, *so I'm not sure what to look for. I just kind of like the idea of someone 'taking charge' in the bedroom.*

Look no further, Velvet replied. *Though I don't do outcalls. And my sex chamber resembles more of a dungeon than a boudoir.*

That sounds kind of scary. Is there any kind of torture or pain involved with your services?

Torture is in the eye of the beholder, she responded. *I inflict just enough pain to elevate your perception of pleasure. The withholding of pleasure can be exquisitely agonizing in its own right. By the time I finish with you, I guarantee you'll reach new heights of ecstasy.*

Just enough pain? Withholding of pleasure? It sounded like she was going to place me in some kind of torture rack. But she definitely had my interest. As I imagined her teasing and punishing me, I unzipped my jeans and thrust my fingers under my panties and began to play with my clit.

What kind of tools and restraints do you use? I typed. *Can I stop it if it gets too intense?*

Not to worry, Velvet replied. *When you arrive at my chamber, we will carefully discuss your interests and boundaries, then your session will be custom-designed to meet your individual needs. All your limits will be respected in a safe, mutually agreed upon way so your enjoyment is guaranteed. We'll sign a mutually binding waiver, and every session will be recorded to ensure everyone's rights are respected.*

Recorded? I suddenly had visions of my kinky S&M session going viral over the internet.

What do you do with the recording? I wouldn't want any of my intimate details being shared with the public...

It's for our mutual protection. I use old-school analog tape, so nothing can be copied. Upon satisfactory completion of the session, the tape is yours to keep. Many of my clients enjoy watching replays of our engagement to relive the moment long after they leave. No other record of the proceedings is taken beyond this.

I paused for a moment. Making a tape actually made a lot of sense. I could see how these sessions could get out of control from both sides, and having a record of the proceedings would ensure quick legal recourse if either party had a grievance. This Mistress Velvet was smart *and* sexy. My hand began moving faster between my legs at the thought of watching myself on videotape with the sexy redhead.

Will I be restrained? I enquired.

Half of the fun of BDSM is not being in control. I have special bondage chairs and harnesses that limit your range of mobility. I will stimulate you with a variety of appendages including whips and feathers and other sensual equipment. Sometimes it's more fun not being able to touch yourself or your partner while the final consumption is withheld.

Whips and feathers? The idea of being teased and tortured by someone while holding off the final release was getting me increasingly worked up. I spread my legs further apart, beginning to feel the pleasure radiating through my body.

Do you leave—marks? I typed with one hand.

Just minor localized inflammation in the form of temporary welts, she said. *I use a special leather whip that doesn't cut the skin. I think you'll find there's nothing like a little pain to heighten the feeling of pleasure.*

I stabbed at the keys while rubbing myself with increasing intensity.

So there'll be opportunities to experience pleasure as well?

Yes, Velvet replied. *It's just that it will be on my terms, and when I choose to allow it.*

Damn. I like the sound of that. I strummed my clit faster at the thought of her bringing me to the height of pleasure, only to make me beg for release.

So I'll be tied up?

Absolutely. I'll have you bound and stretched as wide as your body will allow so I can have my way with you.

Fuck me, I thought. I tore off my jeans and panties and thrust my fingers into my steaming tunnel. This Velvet goddess was already torturing me online.

Will I be able to touch you?

Only insofar as I take the initiative to touch you first. I enjoy touching my clients' bodies and having them touch me. But there will be limited ways in which you'll be able to engage with your hands and your feet while you're bound in the harness.

I smiled at the thought of Velvet having her way with me while I could only watch.

So you get off watching me squirm in restraints?

Absolutely. That's what being the domme is all about. As my slave, your role is to satisfy any of my curiosities and sexual whims. My clients get off just as much watching me get sexually aroused as when they finally have a chance to achieve release themselves.

The thought of watching this sexy redhead pleasure herself while I helplessly looked on elicited the familiar pangs of escalating pleasure from my core.

Do allow your clients to satisfy themselves in the end? I panted, stabbing spastically at the keyboard.

Yes, in a matter of speaking. But I'm the one who's always in control. Your release comes on my terms with my choice of apparatus. I assure you that after an hour of teasing and gentle torturing, your climax will be like no other.

"God! I" gasped, as my orgasm suddenly took hold of me. The image of this sexy redhead fucking me with some kind of contraption while I whimpered for release wrapped up in a ball of chains took me over the edge. I jerked softly in my chair as the waves of passion consumed me, reading what she'd written.

I believe you, I typed, pecking at the keys.

I paused for a moment to consider the next steps.

What are your rates and how soon are you available?

I charge four hundred dollars per hour, with a fifty percent deposit payable on booking and the remainder due at the start of the session. I'm booked solid for this week except for a small window this Saturday between ten a.m. and noon. If you'd like to reserve this spot, please fill in your online profile and complete the credit card details under the bookings tab.

That works for me, I typed. *If you can fit me into your Saturday slot, this is much appreciated.*

I'll block it off pending completion of your payment. May I ask your first name so I'll know who to expect?

I paused, contemplating whether to give her my real name.

It's Jade, I said, using the pseudonym that had become so intimately intertwined with my real identity.

Outstanding, Velvet replied. *Girls are a real treat from my usual parade of uptight guys.*

I smiled, knowing that she had a strong affinity for women.

See you Saturday, Velvet, I typed. *I mean Mistress Velvet,* signing off with a winking kiss emoji.

Saturday morning wasn't the only slot of hers I planned to fit into, I thought, as my juices dripped down over my hand still inserted deep inside my tunnel.

2

———

BONDAGE

On Saturday morning, I drove to Mistress Velvet's studio with a mix of trepidation and excitement. I was intrigued about being with a more dominant sexual partner, but I definitely felt uneasy about the idea of being tied up. As long as I remained in her clutches, I'd be completely at the mercy of someone who professed to enjoy inflicting pain.

As I drove across town, I kept shaking my head, unsure if I wanted to go through with it. I told myself that I'd check out her operation and that if I wasn't feeling entirely comfortable, I'd walk away. We'd have a long conversation about ground rules, and even if it ate into a portion of my paid session time, I needed to be sure I'd have final control over what happened to my body.

But something told me that this dominatrix was far more interested using me for her *own* pleasure than in watching someone else suffer. Anybody who was that concerned about protecting her safety with written contracts and session recordings must have long ago learned where to draw the line. The closer I got to her address, the tighter my thighs squeezed together, pinching my buzzing clit.

When my car's navigation system indicated that I'd arrived at my final designation, I looked around trying to locate Mistress Velvet's storefront. The street address comprised a long strip mall and there was no visible signage revealing her service location. I drove into the half-empty parking lot and stopped my car in front of the indicated unit number. A large plate-glass window covered the storefront with closed horizontal blinds.

Something didn't feel right. Everything was just too quiet and secluded. It would be the perfect location to torture and hold someone captive while you had your way with them. I was just about to turn around and drive away when I saw a young mother and child enter another shop a couple of doors down. I looked up and read the adjacent signs. There was a health clinic and a pet store on either side of the unmarked address. As a steady stream of patrons began to file in and out of the stores, my heart rate slowly returned to normal.

I got out of my car and walked up to the unmarked door to Unit Fourteen. Peering through the glass, I saw the familiar logo of Mistress Velvet dressed up in a naughty bodice riding a unicorn. Near the bottom of the sign was an arrow pointing down a long flight of stairs.

Of course she wouldn't broadcast her services for just any random passerby, I thought. *Who knows what kind of weirdos this kind of operation would attract? This is exactly the kind of service that should be by appointment only.*

I pulled on the handle and found it locked. I squinted at the side of the door and saw a small buzzer with a handwritten note reading *Press for Attendant.* I pressed the button and after a few seconds a female voice responded.

"Hello?" the voice said.

"My name is Jade," I replied. "I have a ten a.m. appointment with Mistress Velvet."

The door clicked and made a loud buzzing sound, and I pulled it open and scampered inside. The place had a strange musky scent, like a gym with slight undertones of lavender. The long flight of stairs led down to a closed door with a larger sign displaying Mistress Velvet's emblem. I walked down the steps and hesitated in front of the heavy door. There was a small peephole at eye height and I rapped on the surface with my knuckles.

A shadow flickered behind the peephole, then the door swung open. The beautiful redhead from Mistress Velvet's website smiled at me wearing a shiny vinyl trench coat with black fishnet stockings and high heels. Her huge breasts thrust against the reflective coating as her long curly locks cascaded over her shoulders. She was even more beautiful in the flesh, with high cheekbones, full pouty lips, and dark penetrating eyes.

"Welcome, Jade," she said, motioning me into the room. "I've been expecting you. Step into my dungeon."

When I entered the room, my eyes opened as wide as saucers. An assortment of whips and chains hung across the exposed brick walls. In each of the four corners rested a strange padded contraption. One could have passed for a conventional massage table, except for the wrist and leg cuffs strapped to either end. In the next corner stood a long padded board balancing on some kind of see-saw apparatus, with long leather straps running across the width of the board in one foot intervals. In the opposite corner rested a tall wooden throne-type chair with metal arm and foot restraints. In the final corner lay some kind of leather harness with a jumble of hopes and chains. Near the middle of the room, a long lever extended up from the floor, directly under a series of hooks and pulleys hanging down from the ceiling. If it weren't for a lone table holding an assortment of dildos and sex toys, I would have thought I was in some kind of medieval torture chamber.

"I see why you call this a *dungeon*," I said, nodding my head slowly. "It looks like more of a torture chamber."

"Everybody's a little taken back the first time they see my sex palace," the redhead nodded. "It looks scarier than it really is. I assure you, everything in this boudoir is designed to take you to new heights of pleasure."

"Only mine?" I said, noticing a huge strap-on dildo resting on the sex toy table.

"That depends on the client," she said, running her eyes up and down my body. "Under the right circumstances, we *both* can have a little fun."

I peered around the room at the assortment of bondage paraphernalia and narrowed my eyes.

"This is my first time doing something like this," I said. "Do you mind if we take a few minutes to discuss exactly what will be involved before we begin?"

"Of course," Velvet nodded. "I'd have it no other way. There are a few necessary preliminaries. Just keep in mind that I have another appointment at eleven. So we'll want to dispense with the formalities as quickly as possible in order to give you the maximum attention you deserve."

"Is there somewhere we can sit down?" I said. "I mean other than the torture rack or the throne chair?"

"Absolutely," Velvet chuckled, motioning in the direction of the sex toy table. "There are some comfortable chairs in this corner."

Velvet opened a collapsible chair and waited for me to sit down before sitting kitty-corner across the table. When she lifted her leg to cross her knees, I caught a fleeting glimpse of a black garter between her legs.

"What concerns do you have that I can assuage?"

"Well, mostly," I began tentatively, "I'm concerned about being tied up and having no ability to—*defend myself*. Will I be able to stop the proceedings at any time if I begin to feel uncomfortable?"

"Of course," she said, batting her long dark eyelashes. "We live in a civilized culture, after all. You'll always have the final say. I'm here to make you feel stimulated and excited, not to inflict unmitigated pain."

"So all I have to do is say 'stop' or 'no' when I want it to stop?"

"Technically, yes. Though I prefer each client to have a more elegant code word to terminate the proceedings. Just keep in mind that if you choose to deny me for any reason, that will automatically end the session and you won't be eligible for any refund of unused time. What would you like your code word to be?"

I paused to think of something less harsh than simply 'stop'.

"How about arrêtez? It means the same thing in French."

"That'll work," Velvet nodded. "But try to use it sparingly, since you can only say it once. I think you may find that the less control you have and the more uncomfortable you feel, the more invigorating the session will be. The whole point of BDSM is in giving complete control to your domme and in embracing the slave role."

My pussy pulsed at the mention of the word slave. I kept staring at the giant strap-on dildo on the other end of our table, thinking what Velvet had in mind for me.

"I understand," I nodded. "Where do we begin?"

Velvet reached into a drawer and passed a piece of paper and a pen across the table.

"I'll just need you to sign this waiver. And your credit card to process the rest of your payment."

"Of course," I said, reaching into my purse and passing her my card.

As Velvet processed my payment, I quickly scanned the contract. It was mostly standard boilerplate, limiting liability in the event of a dispute over the nature of services rendered. I was happy to see the clause referencing the recording of the proceedings and that I would be given the only tape upon successful completion of the session. The contract reiterated that Mistress Velvet would have complete and total authority to do whatever she pleased with me, so long as I didn't utter the agreed upon code word.

"Does everything appear satisfactory?" Velvet said, handing me the credit card voucher to sign.

"Yes, I think so," I said. "Although I'm a little confused by what 'satisfactory completion' of the session means."

"That's more for my protection than yours. It simply means that as long as I'm not physically threatened or harmed, you'll be given possession of the recording upon completion of the session. Not that I'm worried about you. But some of my male clients like to play pretty rough." Velvet pointed to a dark glass window on the far wall of the room. "Until then, everything will be securely filmed behind that wall."

I looked at the dark window and chuckled nervously.

"How do I know there isn't also some weirdo peeping at us behind that wall?"

"Fair question," Velvet said, beckoning me toward the door. "I like to be completely transparent at all times."

She punched in a code on the keypad lock, then swung the door open for me to look inside. I peered into the closet-sized room and saw an old VHS video camera on a tripod, pointed toward the window.

"I like your style, Miss Velvet," I said, appreciating her abundance of caution.

"Shall we begin then?"

"Yes, I feel comfortable now."

Velvet stepped into the video room and pressed a button on the side of the camera and a red light begin to flash. Then she pulled the door closed and we returned to the sex toy table, where I signed the contract.

"Right then," she said, suddenly changing her tone. "From this point forward, you are to address me only as Mistress Velvet or Master. I will refer to you simply as Slave. Repeat the code word that you wish to use to cease all proceedings one last time. In the absence of this code word, you are to obey all of my commands. Is that understood?"

"Yes—Master," I smiled. "The code word is arrêtez."

"Good," Velvet said. "Now strip off all your clothes."

"Everything?"

"Everything."

I unbuttoned my blouse and slowly pulled it off my shoulders.

"Where shall I put them?" I said, looking at Velvet demurely.

"Hand them to me. I'll place them in a safe location."

I handed Velvet my blouse then unclasped my bra and passed it to her. Although she maintained a steely expression as she peered back and forth across my naked breasts, the quickening pace of her breathing as evidenced by her heaving breasts above her corset, betrayed her excitement.

"Now your pants," she ordered, glancing below my waist.

I unzipped my jeans and lowered them slowly to the floor. Then I pulled off my sneakers and handed them to her. Finally, I pulled down my panties and held them out with an outstretched arm.

"What about you?" I said, running my eyes over her curvaceous figure hidden under her trench coat.

"I'm the one giving orders here, slave," she barked. "Now stand still while I appraise your figure."

She ran her eyes up and down my body, pausing for a long moment to stare at my bald hips and mound, then again at my nipples, which seemed to get harder and more erect the longer she stared at them.

"Not too shabby," she said, narrowing her eyes. "Now turn around."

I turned one-hundred-and-eighty degrees and stared at the dark window, smiling for the video camera.

"Spread your legs shoulder width apart and bend over ninety degrees."

As I followed Velvet's command, I felt the moisture beginning to accumulate on the inside of my labia.

"Very nice," she said. "Now turn around and face me again, with your legs spread shoulder width apart."

I turned around, and Velvet lowered her head to gaze at the bare folds of skin outlining my pussy.

"You'll do fine," she said. "I'm going to have a lovely time using and abusing your girlish figure. Wait here while I retrieve your harness."

Velvet hung up my clothes on a hook next to some whips and chains, then she disappeared behind me where I heard some rustling of clothes and equipment. When she returned to face me, she'd taken off her trench coat and was carrying a tangled assortment of leather, ropes, and chains. She kneeled down on the floor and spread out the equipment into a star shape, with the ropes angling out in four directions from a perforated leather harness.

When she stood back up, I ran my eyes wildly over her body. Her

D-cup breasts spilled over the top of a black leather half-corset, with her large brown nipples pointing sensuously toward me above the seam. Her waist tapered to a narrow midsection, before flaring to wide, curvy hips, framed by a crotchless black leather garter supporting fishnet stockings with long thin black straps running up the front of her bare thighs. Her pussy, like mine, was entirely bare, revealing a large nub between her legs. I sagged at my knees, gasping at her gorgeous body.

"Lie down on the harness," Velvet commanded, directing her eyes to the floor.

"Can I just—" I pleaded, wanting a few more seconds to take in her magnificent figure.

"Lie down!" she commanded.

"Yes, Master," I demurred, kneeling down on the floor. "How do you want me—"

"Place your ass at the bottom of the harness, then lie back with your head toward the ropes. I'll take care of the rest."

I did as I was told, lying back against the cold perforated leather. The harness looked like a small hammock with large holes to permit maximum access to the recliner's skin. Velvet kneeled down and straddled my waist, and my pussy throbbed as I envisioned her rubbing herself against me. But instead she reached over my head and grabbed the ropes splayed out on the floor and began wrapping them tightly around my tits. She encircled each breast with the nylon cord, then ran a figure eight across the front of my chest and tied the two ends securely around the back of my neck.

My eyes widened at the thought of having a rope tied around my neck, but I began to relax when I realized the pressure point was behind my shoulders rather than over my throat. I peered down at my tightly bound boobs, noticing how they'd already swelled from the constricted circulation. My areolas had turned a dark shade of purple and my nipples stood out almost a full inch, tingling in arousal.

Velvet paused for a moment to appraise her handiwork then peered into my eyes with a sexy grin.

"Do you like that, my sexy little slave?" she purred. She grabbed my tits with her two hands and squeezed them roughly. "Because your nipples are definitely saying yes."

"Yes," I squeaked, arching my hips to press against her body.

Velvet spread her knees wider apart, placing her full weight on my abdomen, thumping my body back onto the floor. Then she lowered her head and sucked hard on each of my erect nipples for a few seconds, making a loud popping sound each time she removed her mouth. Her wet pussy writhed against my bare stomach as she pinned her body over mine.

"Fuck yes!" I exclaimed, letting her know in no uncertain terms that I was enjoying her attention.

Then she shimmied her hips over my hard mound and hipbones, spreading her juices over my midsection like she was marking me.

"I'm going to have a lot of fun with you before we're finished," she said. "But first I need to get you properly restrained so I can have my way with you."

She waddled up my body until her pussy rested just above my face, then she grabbed my arms and tied the ropes at the top of the harness tightly around my wrists. Then she threaded the loose ends through two eyelets and tied secure knots to hold my arms high above my head. When she finished binding my hands to the harness, she peered down to see me staring at her glistening labia. I extended my tongue trying to touch her throbbing clit, but she kneeled just far enough away for me not to reach her.

"You want to lick my pussy, slave?" she taunted. "You'll have to beg for it. But don't worry, there will be plenty of opportunities for you to satisfy me soon enough. Let's get those pretty little legs of yours pulled up with your arms. I want to have unfettered access to your sweet, moist kitty."

Velvet lifted her knee and turned around so she was straddling me in the other direction. She leaned forward, revealing her pink rosebud and dripping labia. When I lifted my head trying to reach her, she shifted her body in the other direction, toward my hips. She paused for a moment over my bound breasts and rubbed her pussy over each of my distended nipples until both of my tits were thoroughly coated with her sex juices. There was something incredibly sexy about her spreading her wetness all over my prostrated body while I could only stand there and watch. My hips twisted and convulsed, trying vainly to produce some friction against my aching clit.

When she reached my midsection, she straddled my hips again and titled forward at the waist, giving me another premium view of her tight rosebud and wide-open lips. Then she grabbed my legs and wound the other two ends of the loose ropes around my ankles while spreading my legs apart. When she finished, she stood up and pulled the ropes as far as she could toward my head, binding my ankles to my hands. I was now stretched as far into an accordion position as my body allowed, with my legs splayed and pulled behind my head. I looked between my legs and saw that my pussy was wide open, with my labia spread apart and my juices dripping down the crack of my ass.

"Now we're talking," Velvet smiled, standing over me, nodding approvingly. "It looks like you're already getting excited about the idea of being hog-tied for my amusement. But you haven't seen anything yet."

She stood over me for a moment, straddling my waist in her six-inch stilettos, then stepped slowly up toward my head. I peered nervously out of the corner of my eyes, fearing she might pinch my skin with her sharp heels, but she simply sneered as she got closer and closer to my breasts. When she reached my armpits, she spread her legs on either side of my shoulders and paused to let me peer up her long and magnificent body. Her legs seemed to go on forever, and above the sensuous cleft between her legs, her tits jutted out like ripe melons from the dark stem of her corset.

Her pussy was glistening in obvious excitement, and as I watched her juices begin to run down the inside of her thighs, I hoped they might eventually reach the sides of my body. But just as I envisioned she might let me have a small taste of her body, she stepped over my head and grabbed the top of my harness and fastened three chains with hooks to the top and two sides of my harness. Then she lifted the three ends of the chains toward a large metal hook hanging from the ceiling.

"What the—?" I muttered, realizing she intended to lift me up onto the hook.

"That's right," Velvet sneered. "I'm going to hang you from the rafters like a piece of meat. Then you'll really see who's in charge here."

She connected the ends of each chain to the large overhead hook, then she grabbed the lever poking up from the floor and began thrusting it forward and back. The slack in the chains tightened, and I began to feel myself lifting off the floor. Most of my weight was supported by the black leather harness, but I could definitely feel my arms and legs stretched tighter and wider with each pull of the lever. When my ass elevated to Velvet's hip level, she stopped cranking the lever and looked down at me. Every part of my body was pulled as high and far apart as possible. I peered down my midsection, seeing my tits squeezed into tight pyramids and my hips curled up toward my face, revealing the separated parts of my puffy lips spread into a wide and gleaming crevasse.

Velvet reached up onto the two chains supporting the sides of my harness and suddenly pulled them down, angling my body forty-five degrees forward.

"Do you like that, my sweet?" she said, looking deep into my eyes, stepping forward and rubbing her bare mound tantalizingly against my splayed pussy.

"Yes, Master," I said. "Please fuck me now. I want you to have your way with me."

"Oh I will, my slave. Don't you worry. When I'm finished with you, I'll have sprayed myself all over your tight little body and you'll have licked every square inch of me."

Velvet walked slowly around my suspended body until she was standing behind my head. Then she reached up and yanked down on the chain supporting the other end of my harness. I suddenly tilted forty-five degrees in the other direction, until my head dangled just under her dripping pussy. Then she turned around and planted her ass on my face.

"Lick my rosebud, slave," she commanded. "I want you to clean me with your tongue."

3

DOMINATION

For a moment, I panicked. I imagined Mistress Velvet subjecting me to an increasingly demeaning series of sex acts where I'd have no ability to extract myself from my helpless state. My face was buried in the cleft of her ass and I had very little freedom of movement. I considered twisting my head and crying out my safe word, but then I remembered the contract said my session would end as soon as I did. I'd signed up for this crazy idea; the least I could do was give her a chance to explore my limits.

Besides, her anus didn't smell nearly as bad as I thought. In fact, it smelled kind of pleasant, with hints of lemongrass and vanilla. Velvet had obviously already cleaned herself with some kind of scented soap.

Of course, I thought, *she wouldn't make someone lick her unclean ass. That would be a little over the top. This was a business after all, and her success relied in large part upon repeat business.*

"What's the matter, slave?" Velvet said, rubbing her cheeks against my face. "Have you never licked a beautiful woman's rosebud before? You never know if you might like it until you try. Don't worry—I won't bite. It's time to pay tribute to your master and kiss my ass."

I tentatively extended my tongue and felt the fleshy folds on the insides of her cheeks. It was soft and smooth, not rough and gritty like I imagined. There was no appreciable taste other than the slightly salty flavor of fresh sweat that I'd experienced while running on the treadmill at the gym. Beyond the faint smell of lemony soap, the only scent that penetrated my nostrils was a sexy musk aroma, similar to the pleasant smell of a woman's freshly washed pussy.

"That's right, sweetheart," Velvet purred. "Lick my ass. Run your tongue over my rosebud and make your master feel good."

I titled my head up a few degrees, moving my tongue closer to her anus. The closer I got to her puckered hole, the more I could feel the gentle folds of her skin on my sensitive tongue. When I reached the deepest part of her pit, I closed my eyes and pursed my lips to prevent the intrusion of any undesired elements. But to my surprise, there was no change in taste or smell, and I found myself enjoying the sensation of probing her most intimate parts with my tongue. Before long, I was swirling and lapping up her bare flesh like an ice cream cone.

"Now you've got the idea," Velvet panted, as she pressed her ass down further and began to hump my face. "Be a good little slave and lick my ass all the way from my tailbone to my pussy."

As Velvet tilted her hips up and down, giving me freer access to the full length of her undersides, I opened my mouth and savored the sexy mixture of my saliva and her bodily fluids coating her ass. Every few seconds, she'd angle her hips far enough forward to allow me to see her rubbing her clit furiously with her right hand. Seeing her touch herself while I licked her most sensitive areas sent a charge through me, and I buried my face deeper into her chasm as I motor-boated her tight ass cheeks.

"Yeah baby," Velvet moaned. "That's what I'm talking about. Have your way with my ass. Make Mistress Velvet cum all over your face."

My eyes suddenly flung open in surprise.

She was going to let me make her cum this way?

This bondage thing had already exceeded my expectations. The feeling of pleasuring my partner while balled up in restraints suspended from the ceiling was more erotic than I ever imagined.

When Velvet shifted her ass down my face and positioned her soaking pussy over my mouth, I moaned into her crevasse.

"Do you like that, slave?" she said. "Do you like burying your face in my sweet pussy? Lick my cunt and taste my juices. Hold still while I fuck your tongue with my slit."

I extended my tongue as far as I could into her hole, curling it to make it firmer and harder. She began to flex her knees up and down, and I penetrated her deeper. Her labia spread wider and wider apart until my entire mouth and chin was embedded in her cavern.

"Fuck, yes," Velvet moaned. "Fuck my pussy with your tongue. Make Mistress Velvet gush all over your pretty face."

As the pace of Velvet's movement on my face increased with the volume of her commands, I knew it wouldn't be long before she came. I pressed my tongue deeper inside her, trying to reach her G-spot. Suddenly, she tilted her hips down and I felt a fleshy proboscis snap into my mouth. For a moment, I was unsure what she had inserted into me until I felt the telltale throbbing of firm flesh.

It was her clitoris. She had a huge, oversized clit. It must have been almost three inches long, and freestanding like a man's cock. Firm and pointy, it felt like a red chili pepper in my mouth. I'd never seen or felt a woman's clit like this, and as I sucked it deeper into my mouth, my own clit pulsed in excitement.

"Yeah, baby," Velvet moaned. "Suck Momma's big cock. Do you like my big fat clit?"

"Umm-hmm," I murmured, wrapping my tongue around the shaft and head-banging her with my face.

"Suck it, slave," Velvet panted. "Suck my flute until I come. I'm getting close."

I could feel her juices streaming all over my face as she face-fucked me with her meaty phallus. I opened my eyes and saw her butt cheeks shaking in a spasm above me and knew that she was close. I began flicking my tongue over the sensitive end of her big clit, then she pulled out of me and planted her ass over my mouth.

"Fuck, yes!" she screamed. "Tease my anus while I come. Make your master cum, slave!"

As I flicked my tongue over her puckered opening, I watched with amazement as her hips writhed and shook over top of me. Her anus seemed to open slightly, and for a moment I worried that she intended to defecate on me in a final perverted denouement to our session. But instead, she pressed down harder onto my face and in one final thrust, let out a primal scream.

"Uhnnn," she groaned. "Fuck my anus, baby. Fuck my hole while I cum all over you."

I curled my tongue again and Velvet pressed it into her hole as her hips and buttocks shook in spastic delirium. To my surprise, I still didn't taste or smell any sign of unpleasantness, as I realized that she'd cleansed her insides also. I peered down between her cheeks and saw her long pointy clit flicking up and down in spastic jerks, like a man does when he comes. The multiple assault on my senses was simply too much, and I suddenly gushed a geyser out of my upturned pussy as I came hard watching and feeling her come.

"Oh! Oh! Oh!" Velvet moaned, as I felt her anus clamping down over my tongue in repeated contractions. This was something I'd never shared with anyone before, and I spasmed along with her for many long seconds before I felt my juices running back down along my elevated thighs and upturned ass. Velvet jerked and moaned with my face still buried in her ass, and I dribbled like a baby as my saliva and her pussy juices washed all over my face.

My first experience with bondage and domination felt more like a baptism than a persecution.

4

DENIAL

When Velvet finally finished cumming, she turned around and grabbed the sides of my head with two hands and pulled my face roughly into her snatch. I peered up at her still-erect clit with wide eyes, amazed at the size of her twitching womanhood.

"Good job, slave," she said. "You're a natural at this. You know how to give good head. Do you like my big girl-cock?"

"Yes," I murmured under the slick folds of her throbbing pussy.

"Do you want me to *fuck* you with it later?"

As I nodded my head enthusiastically, my pussy pushed out one last spasm of love nectar. Velvet peered up and noticed the coating of juices over my legs, then she narrowed her gaze and shook her head disapprovingly.

"What's that?" she said. "You didn't come too, did you? Because I haven't given my permission. You're only supposed to satisfy *me*."

"I'm sorry," I said. "I couldn't help it. It was just too much of a turn-on watching you—"

"*I'm* the one who decides when you're allowed to feel any pleasure. You've been a naughty girl, and now you'll have to pay the price for breaking the rules."

Velvet paced to the far wall where she removed some items hanging on the hooks on the exposed brick surface, then she lifted a collapsed director's chair and placed it on the floor in front of me. She unfolded the chair and placed the paraphernalia on the seat, then reached down and lifted two stainless steel clasps and held them up in front of my face.

"You'll have to experience a little bit of pain to pay amends for stealing some unauthorized pleasure. Do you know what these are?"

"Um," I hesitated, looking at the devices with wide eyes. "I can guess—"

"That's right," she said. "They're nipple clamps. This will teach you what it feels like to disobey your master."

Velvet pressed the front of my harness down a few inches as my head tilted toward the floor. Then she squeezed the clasps open one at a time and placed them over my erect nipples and slowly spread her fingers. As the pressure of the clamps squeezed tighter and tighter against my nipples, I groaned in pain.

"Does that hurt, baby?" Velvet said in a taunting voice. "Don't worry, you'll get used to it soon enough. You might even grow to like it. Many of my clients find the pain only heightens the pleasurable feeling of being bound and controlled."

I grimaced as I watched my nipples turn a ruddy shade of purple from the constricted circulation. But inside, I had to admit seeing the metal clamps standing firmly attached to my erect nipples was turning me on even more.

"But don't get too excited about having your erogenous parts stimulated," she said. "Because I have so many other ways to punish you."

Velvet grabbed the side of my harness and swung me around one-hundred-and-eighty degrees until my ass was facing her once again. Then she pulled the front of the harness down so I was tilted up just enough for me to see her midsection. As I watched her still-throbbing woman-cock, for a moment I thought she intended to fuck me with it to teach me a lesson. But instead, she sat down on the director's chair and picked up a long wand that looked like some kind of horse whip. Staring between my legs, she snapped it in the air in front of my exposed pussy.

"That's a very pretty kitty you have," she said. "What kind of implements do you think it might accommodate for me today? I have such a broad selection of equipment..."

Velvet slapped the leather strands at the end of the wand on top of my chest, and I flinched as I watched the strands splay out across my breasts.

"Did that hurt, baby?" she said, pinching her eyebrows together in mock empathy. "Because we're just getting started."

She slowly pulled the whip down the front of my body until the leather strands ran between my legs and spilled over my pussy. I shuddered at the first sensation of direct contact against my private parts and raised my hips begging for more.

"Do you like that?" Velvet said, raising an eyebrow.

She raised the whip over her head and held it menacingly over my quivering snatch. Then she suddenly arced the wand to the side of my hips and snapped the leather straps against the bottom of the harness. I yelped when I felt the sting of the straps on my bare ass through the holes in the harness and instinctively tilted my hips in the other direction.

"Sorry," Velvet teased. "I didn't mean to strike you quite so—*softly*."

She snapped the whip again and struck me a few inches lower on my buttocks on the same side of the harness. I winced in pain and twisted the harness as far as I could away from her.

"There's nowhere you can go, my sweet," she said with a sneer. "You're just going to have to lie there and take your punishment. But don't worry, my whips are specially designed to inflict maximum pain with minimum bodily harm. This is an equestrian whip, designed with wide, smooth-edged strands of leather that won't puncture your skin. Doesn't it feel sublime?"

Velvet shifted the wand to her other hand and suddenly snapped the whip against the other side of my body. My body jerked from the unexpected attack on my unblemished side.

"I can't hear you," Velvet said, snapping the whip in the same area, stinging my left buttock cheek.

"Yes, Mistress," I groaned weekly.

Velvet snapped the whip harder, striking me on the same tender part that was still smarting from her last lash.

"Yes, Master," I squealed, louder.

I struggled to form the right words to describe the sensation.

"It feels...tender, yet sensitive. I see what you mean by heightening my sensations."

A wide smile formed on Velvet's lips.

"Exactly. Doesn't the pain so close to your most sensitive zones make you tingle all the more in other areas?"

"Yes Master," I said, unsure if by agreeing it would be more likely to increase or decrease her flogging.

"Well then, let's finish getting you properly tenderized. It will make the next stage all the more enjoyable."

"For you or for me?" I said, wondering what she had in store next.

"Silence!" Velvet barked. "I'll tell you when you can speak. Speak now!"

She snapped the whip three times in rapid succession against the underside of my harness, each time getting closer and closer to my exposed pussy. Each time I squealed out loud, half in real pain and half in overreaction, hoping she'd have mercy and strike me more softly.

For another minute or so, she struck me repeatedly, flogging the entire underside of my back and buttocks, until she leaned over and placed the whip on the floor. I was glad that she'd spared my front side, not least because my breasts were already tender from the clamps still pinching my tender and extended nipples.

Velvet glanced up at the clock on the adjacent wall, then reached down beside her chair to pick up a new object that was outside my line of sight. It was ten-forty. I couldn't imagine another twenty minutes of this kind of punishment before our session ended.

"Have you learned your lesson, slave?" she said. "Do you think you've felt enough pain for today?"

"Yes, Mistress," I said, wondering what she intended to do with our remaining time.

"Alright then," she said, suddenly standing up. She lifted her arm and waved a long feather boa in the air. "Let's see if we can torment you with a different kind of pain. Sometimes it's the softest of touches that can be the most cruel."

Velvet lowered the boa toward the floor and traced it along the sides of the harness as she walked slowly around my suspended body. I shivered at the soft sensation of the feather against the tender welts where she'd flogged me with the whip. When she reached the other side of my body, she placed the feather at the top of my head and slowly lowered it over my face. I closed my eyes, feeling the soft fringes flow over my cheeks and jaw, raising my chest instinctively to welcome it on the lower portion of my body. When she reached my neck, she angled the boa sideways and drew it across my throat in both directions. The feathers tickled me slightly, and I giggled softly.

"It tickles, does it?" Velvet said, smiling at me gently. "Maybe this will tickle your fancy even more."

She dragged the large boa slowly over my chest, stopping to encircle each of my clamped nipples with the most delicate touch. I arched my back, enjoying the exquisite softness juxtaposed against my stinging nipples enclosed in the tight clamps.

"There now," Velvet purred. "Doesn't that feel better? Mistress Velvet isn't all about pain, you know. Don't you agree that pleasant feelings are magnified in the presence of pain?"

"Yes," I sighed, rolling my breasts across the feather to increase the stimulation.

"Shall we test this theory by stimulating your more erogenous areas now?" she said, glancing in the direction of my upturned pussy.

"Yes please," I panted, tilting my aching pussy further up in the air.

Velvet chuckled as she moved the boa onto the undersides of my upturned legs. Then she slowly waved it down my thighs toward my throbbing snatch. Even though my back and buttocks were still smarting from the flogging she'd just meted out, the feeling of the soft feather on my untouched skin made the little hairs on my legs stand up in excitement. It was true what she'd said about pleasurable sensations being magnified in the presence of pain.

But when the boa reached the base of my thighs, instead of drawing it inward toward my pussy, she tilted her arm and drew it softly across my back. The feeling of the soft feather touching my painful welts somehow multiplied the tenderness of my skin, and I grimaced as she fluttered it over the inflamed surface.

"It's strange feeling pleasure and pain at the same time, isn't it?" Velvet said, smiling at my discomfort.

I nodded softly, not wanting to encourage her too much.

"Let's see if it feels any better on the untouched parts of your body," she said.

She dragged the feather along the underside of my body toward my buttocks, then drew it up between the crack of my ass and over my pussy. She watched my legs quivering as my pussy dribbled down my crease.

"Yes," Velvet smiled, noticing the wetness between my legs. "Your body seems to agree. Are those cries of sadness or pleasure?"

"Pleasure," I whimpered, as she tilted her hand up and down, drawing the feather up and down my folds. I wriggled my hips wildly, trying to increase the friction of the feather against my burning clit, but Velvet seemed to enjoy steering it just at the edge of my love button.

"Please," I blurted out, forgetting that I wasn't supposed to speak unless spoken to.

"Do you want *more*?" Velvet said, smiling at me with a sinister sneer. "Or would you like something a little *firmer* touching your pretty little twat?"

"Yes please," I nodded enthusiastically.

"Let's see if we can find something a little more—*satisfying*."

She leaned over and picked a new object off the seat of the director's chair. When she held it up for me to see, my eyes widened and my pussy pulsed uncontrollably. It was a Magic Wand, one of my favorite vibrating sex toys.

"You've used one of these before, I see," she said, plugging the device into an extension cord snaking from the wall.

I nodded softly, twisting my hips in a beckoning motion.

"Perhaps not quite the way I intend to use it though," she said.

Velvet flicked the ON switch on the side of the handle and the ball-shaped head of the vibrator began to buzz and shake. Then she leaned over and held the vibrating head against each of my nipple clamps. I gasped at the sensation of the snaps buzzing against my tender nubs.

"Pleasure and pain," Velvet smiled, looking into my eyes. "Isn't it exquisite?"

I nodded excitedly, rolling my body in excited convolutions.

"Something tells me you might like it even more somewhere *else*," she said, glancing at my twitching pussy.

She pressed the head of the wand against the underside of my knee and slowly traced it down my right thigh until it hovered next to my quivering labia. As I felt the vibrations radiating into my core, I twisted my hips to press the vibrator closer to my aching clit.

"Do you want more *direct* contact?" Velvet teased, peering into my eyes.

"Yes, Master," I moaned. "Please—Mistress."

"Your wish is my command."

She slowly lowered the vibrator until it sat between the crack of my ass, then she pulled it forward until it rested over my anus. Feeling the vibrations directly against my rosebud while my pussy quivered in excitement was something I'd never experienced before. I began to feel the familiar urge rising up inside me and could have easily come from the stimulation to this sensitive area of my perineum, but Velvet suddenly lifted the wand off my skin when she noticed my breathing escalate.

"You see?" she said. "The anus is indeed an erogenous zone. It's not just *guys* who like to have that area stimulated. But it's too early to let you release all that pent-up energy. I have other plans for you."

I turned my head to glance at the clock on the wall. It read ten-fifty-five. There was only five minutes left in my scheduled session, and I was aching to come.

"Please, Mistress," I begged. "Let me come. I'm burning up inside."

Velvet sat down on the director's chair and lifted her thighs over the armrests, spreading her bare pussy apart.

"Is *this* what you want?" she said.

She placed the head of the magic wand over her slit then rubbed it up and down her opening, pausing for a long moment to stimulate her anus, then she pulled it back up and inserted the thick ball inside her dripping pussy. As she wiggled her hips and moaned softly, I watched her clit once again rise and extend from her body. When it had reached its full three-inch hard angry state, she pulled the vibrator out of her pussy and pressed it firmly against her twitching digit with two hands.

"Do you think you can come again, watching me get off?" she asked, peering at me through dewy eyes. "Because I'd like to watch you gush all over your thighs and ass while I come."

I shook my head, unsure if I could come again without direct stimulation. But the sight of Velvet jilling herself with two hands on the vibrating wand held against her big chili pepper clit, soon changed my mind. Within seconds, I felt the familiar pangs of a rising orgasm welling up within me, and I tilted my head to look at my twitching pussy lips.

"Yes, Master," I groaned. "I'll happily come with you."

"Good," she said. "This time I'm going to watch your rosebud pucker and spasm when you come. I'm getting close. Are you ready?"

"Yes," I panted, feeling the first waves of my orgasm beginning to wash over me. "I'm going to cum, Master."

"Uhnnn," Velvet moaned. "Cum with me, baby. Let me see your sweet hole smile and pucker for me. Here it comes!"

Velvet suddenly screamed out my name as her arm muscles tightened and she began jerking wildly in her chair.

"Jade!" she yelled. "Spray your cum all over your master's tits and cock. I'm cumming!"

As soon as Velvet uttered those words, I lost all control and my pussy and anus began clamping down hard, as all the built-up fluid inside my upturned pussy sprayed out in a wide arc directly in front of Velvet. As she spasmed in her chair, my juices spread all over her giant tits and girl-cock. For almost a full minute, the two of us faced each other, thrashing and moaning while we watched each other have one of the most powerful orgasms of our lives.

5

CONSUMMATION

After Velvet finally stopped cumming in her chair, she stood up and walked over to me. She placed her palms on the underside of my upturned legs then drew her hands down over my dripping skin and smeared my juices all over her breasts. As if winking at me, her big pink clit still stood on end, twitching between her legs.

"You're been a good girl," she said. "You know how to satisfy Mistress Velvet like a proper slave."

She noticed me glancing at her huge clit and smiled.

"But something tells me you're still not satisfied. Do you want something inside that pretty pussy to feel like a complete woman?"

"Yes," I said, peering up at the wall clock. It was two minutes before eleven. The last thing I needed was another client walking in and seeing me hanging in the air covered with my own sex juices.

"But aren't you expecting—"

"There's been a cancellation. I've got another free hour if you'd like to use it. I'm willing to offer it for half the regular rate if you're interested."

Whether she'd told me earlier that she had another appointment to encourage me to take the last open slot of the week, didn't matter to me. Right now, I desperately needed to be fucked, and I would have paid twice the going rate if she'd demanded it.

"I'm definitely interested," I panted, swiveling my hips in front of her fluttering clit.

"Good," she said. "We can take care of the payment at the end of the session. Was there anything in particular you had in mind?"

I licked my lips as I stared at her giant twitching pudendum.

"I want you to fuck me with your big girl-cock," I said, spilling out my fantasy.

"I bet you do," Velvet said. "You've never been fucked by a real ladycock, have you?"

At this point, I was hardly in a position to quibble about whether any of my previous transgender experiences qualified.

"No," I said. "Please fuck me, Mistress Velvet. I want to feel you inside me while I cum all over your pretty clit."

Velvet hesitated for a moment while she ran her eyes over my bound-up body.

"We might be able to arrange that," she said. "But first, I want you to suck me. Let's see what kind of head my pretty slave can muster up for her master."

She swung the harness around again until my face was between her legs. Her vulva was slick with a mixture of our juices, and her large erect clit waved in the air above my mouth.

"First, I want to fuck your throat to remind you who's the master. If you're a good slave and make me cum hard enough, we'll see about filling that pretty little pussy of yours with an appropriate tool."

I was disappointed that she wasn't going to fuck me yet with her big clit, but I was excited about the prospect of feeling it inside my mouth. She stepped forward until she was standing directly over my face, then she tilted my head downwards and forced my jaw open. Then she thrust her wet chili pepper all the way into my cavity.

At first, I almost choked on the sudden intrusion, but when I realized that her cock wasn't long enough to touch the back of my throat, I relaxed and closed my lips around the shaft. It was strange feeling the pointy phallus in my mouth. It was thinner and shorter than other cocks I'd had, and it was comforting to know that she couldn't gag me with it or fill my mouth with salty cum. I wrapped my tongue around the fleshy stem and bobbed my head against her undercarriage, trying my best to give her a memorable blowjob.

"That's my girl," Velvet said. "Suck your master's girl-cock. Feel me twitching inside your pretty mouth."

She grabbed the sides of my head and pulled me harder against her vulva and began thrusting her cock deeper inside my mouth. Far from feeling used, there was something incredibly sexy about feeling another woman's wet vulva mashing against my face while she fucked my mouth like a man. As Velvet thrust her cock deeper inside me, I pursed my lips to increase the pressure on her shaft and began to swirl my lips around the pointed end.

"Fuck yes," Velvet panted. "Suck the head of my dick, slave. Just like that. Make your master cum in your mouth."

She tilted her hips down a few degrees to press deeper inside me, and I opened my eyes to see her buttocks spreading apart, revealing her twitching rosebud. As she increased the speed of her thrusting into my mouth, I could see her hole widening as she approached climax. I found it fascinating to watch this previously unexplored organ go through the same cycle of arousal, plateau, and orgasm that I was so familiar with from my own pussy.

Velvet's commands suddenly elevated in pitch and urgency, and I knew she was on the edge.

"Yes, Jade," she moaned. "I'm going to cum inside your pretty mouth.

"Ohhhh!" she suddenly groaned.

Although she wasn't cumming inside me like a regular man, there was no doubt that she was in the throes of a real orgasm, as I watched her pretty pucker spasm and clench in repeated strong contractions.

"Uh-Uh-Uh," she panted in synchronicity with each of her contractions.

I sucked as hard as I could on her twitching cock while she gushed all over my face and neck. The feeling of being prostrated underneath her while she had her way with me just added to the eroticism of the experience. Though I didn't come with her this time, my pussy throbbed and pulsed in sympathy with each of her contractions. I could feel myself leaking once again out my slit, and in my reclined state, my juices began running down my stomach and over my tightly bound breasts.

Velvet kept hold of my head, jerking softly against my face, until her rosebud finally stopped spasming, then she pulled out of me and held her twitching clit over my eyes. I watched in fascination as the pointy appendage jerked and throbbed with each new beat of her heart. She held herself over me for a moment, running her eyes all over my upturned body, nodding in approval.

"That was heavenly," she panted, still out of breath. "You sure know how to give good head, little girl. I think it's time you had a proper reward."

She peered up my body at my twitching hole.

"Are you ready to see what it feels like to have a big girl-cock inside your pussy now?"

"Yes, master," I said. "I'm so ready for you to fuck me."

"So am I," Velvet said. "I want to bury my dick deep in your cunny. Are you ready for me to fuck you like a man now?"

"Yes, master. Fuck me with your man-cock."

Velvet swung the harness around again, then angled it down until my hips were just under hers. I tilted my head up and was glad to have a clear line of sight all the way down her upper thighs. But instead of stepping forward and inserting her ladycock into my hole, she turned around and leaned over to wiggle her ass in my face.

What is it with this anal obsession of hers? I thought. As sexy as it was, I need some direct stimulation. *If she doesn't trib me or fuck me right now, I'll go out of my mind.*

As if reading my mind, Velvet suddenly lowered her hips onto mine and began swiping her wet lips over mine.

"God, yes," I moaned. "Rub your pussy against me, Miss Velvet. That feels so good."

"Mmm, yes," Velvet purred. "You're so wet. Your lips are so soft and puffy. Have you been getting pumped up watching Mistress Velvet having her way with you?"

"Yes," I panted. "I've been throbbing the whole time I've watched you. I'm ready to burst at the seams."

"I like the sound of that. Will you gush inside your master's pussy this time? I want to feel you spray all over my ass when you cum."

"Fuck yes," I moaned. "I'm gonna squirt all over your pretty rosebud."

Velvet tilted her hips toward me, and I felt her clit slip inside me.

"Yes, master," I squealed, thrilled to finally feel her inside me. "Fuck me with your big ladycock."

As Velvet began humping my hips up and down, I tilted my head forward to watch her pointy appendage pistoning inside me. The feeling of having her hot clit inside me while she mashed her pussy lips against mine felt sublime. I'd been holding off for so long feeling any direct stimulation on my pussy that it didn't take long for the passion to quickly well up inside me.

"Mistress Velvet," I moaned. "You're going to make me cum soon. I can't hold it any longer. Fuck me hard with your big cock."

Velvet picked up the pace of her pounding against my vulva, then she tilted her hips down a bit further and I felt the tip of her pointy cock tickling my G-spot. My orgasm suddenly crashed over me with the power of a tsunami.

"Fuck, yes!" I screamed. "I'm cumming! Pound me, Mistress Velvet. Pound my sweet pussy while I cum all over your pretty cock and ass."

I tensed my neck muscles to keep my head tilted forward and watched a geyser erupt from my upturned pussy as I sprayed all over Velvet's tight pucker.

"Oh God," she screamed. "I feel you cumming all over my ass."

As she pressed her hips against me with one final thrust, her buttock muscles twitched and spasmed as she jerked her hips force-fully against mine. With each strong contraction of my orgasm, I sprayed four or five powerful squirts directly up the crack of her ass. My juices bounced off her buttocks and redirected over the front of my body, reaching as far as my face a couple of times. I wailed and thrashed my hips against Velvet as she held her long clit inside me for many long seconds. When we finally came down from our highs, she pulled her appendage out of me then she turned around and licked all the way up my vulva from my anus to my clit.

"That was good, baby," she said, winking at me with a sly smile. "Did you enjoy having your master's cock inside you?"

"Yes," I panted. "Thank you, master. I really needed that. Thank you for letting me come."

"It was my pleasure, believe me," she said, glancing up at the clock. "But we still have almost a full half hour left in your session. What shall we do with you with your remaining time?"

I looked at her with wide eyes, shaking my head. Whatever it was, I hoped it would involve more of this type of pleasure than the previous pain.

Velvet peered at my twitching pussy and paused. Then she steepled her fingers together and inserted her hand all the way into my hole up to her knuckles.

"As much as I enjoyed fucking you with my girl-cock," she said, "something tells me you're used to having *bigger* objects inside your tight cunny. Are you ready for a real man-sized cock now?"

I pinched my eyes at Velvet, unsure what she meant.

"No—I don't have a real man standing by to pleasure you," she laughed. "But I might have the next best thing."

She walked over to the far wall and lifted a blanket off a long piece of furniture nestled behind the throne chair. It was a square box with a long shaft extending horizontally out the end, with a giant dildo attached to the end. She grasped the metal shaft with one hand and tilted the box up on its end, then rolled it over in front of me.

"Have you ever tried one of these?" she said. "It's a fucking machine. My clients find it can be quite satisfying once they're properly warmed up. Do you think you can accommodate a slightly larger penis inside you?"

I looked at the giant dildo attached to the end of the rod and shook my head.

"That's a mighty big penis," I said. "How exactly does that thing work?"

"I'm sure you've experienced plenty bigger cocks than mine before," Velvet sneered. "It works just like a man does, providing forward thrust and pumping action. Let me show you."

Velvet pulled the device closer to my body, then strolled over to the handle in the middle of the floor. She pushed it away from her a few times, and my body ratcheted closer to the floor. When my pussy was about level with the height of the sex machine shaft, she returned to the box and flipped a switch on its upper surface. The metal bar began slowly pushing in and out of the box as the dildo thrust inches away from my dripping pussy.

My body instinctively turned away from the automated device as my eyes widened in fear. I wasn't quite ready to be fucked by a machine over which I had little control. Besides, the phallus attached to the end of the pushrod had to be at least ten inches long and three inches thick. I wasn't even sure it could fit inside me.

"What do you think, slave?" Velvet taunted. "Are you ready to be dominated by a new kind of master?"

"I'm not sure," I said, tentatively. "Exactly how deep and fast does this thing go?"

"That's entirely up to *me*," she said, lifting a remote-control device off the top lid and thumbing the control wheel forward.

As Velvet's smile grew progressively wider, the dildo began pumping faster and faster. Although my head was shaking no, my pussy was spilling a steady stream of love juices all over my ass.

"At least *one* part of you seems to like the idea," she said, noticing the cataract running between my legs. "Are you ready to give it a try?"

I nodded my head slowly, and Velvet pulled the device closer to me until the tip of the phallus was pressed against the entrance to my hole. Then she sat back on her chair and inched the flywheel forward with her thumb. I felt the dildo press harder against my opening, pressing my lips wider apart. Slowly, it inched further forward, spreading me wider apart. My eyes widened as I watched the huge cock slowly slide inside me until it was buried to the hilt. I moaned as it filled me up, surprised I could take its full length and girth.

"There now," Velvet said. "Doesn't it feel better to have a full-sized man cock inside you? Are you ready to be properly fucked now?"

"Yes," I nodded slowly.

I still wasn't sure I was ready to be fucked by such an imposing device while being tied up and in complete lack of control. But then I remembered I could utter my safe word at any time and stop the proceedings. Besides, Velvet would ultimately be in control of the device, and so far, she'd demonstrated reasonable restraint in subjecting me to unpleasant acts.

She pushed the control wheel forward, and the dildo began slowly pushing in and out of me. The silicone composition of the phallus made it soft and pliant, making it feel like a real man's penis. Before long, I began lubricating more freely and swaying my hips in tandem with the dildo's movement.

"I see you like being fucked by a *man*-cock too," Velvet smiled. "It looks like you swing both ways. Are you enjoying being filled up by a life-size penis?"

"Yes," I panted, feeling the big dildo spreading me open with each new thrust. "Fuck me with your man-cock, Mistress Velvet."

Velvet pressed the control wheel further forward, increasing the thrusting speed of the dildo. As I began writhing and moaning in my harness from the rising pleasure between my legs, Velvet placed her free hand around her erect clit and began jerking it up and down like a man.

"Fuck yes," I said, watching her get off watching me being fucked by her robot proxy. "Rub your big clit for me. I want to watch you cum again while I get fucked by this big cock."

Velvet slid down in her chair and spread her legs further apart as she thumbed the wheel forward another inch. The big dildo was now pistoning rapidly inside me, and I arched my back preparing to cum.

"Velvet," I panted. "Fuck me with your robot cock. I'm going to cum soon. Pound me harder."

Velvet pressed the flywheel forward as far as it could go as the dildo began cavitating rapidly inside me. With her mouth opened wide and her eyes glazed over, I knew she was on the precipice with me.

"Cum, baby," I said, temporarily forgetting the protocol of master and slave communications. "Let me see your pretty clit twitch and jerk with your orgasm."

Velvet removed her hand from her cocklet and she arched her back as she lifted her hips in the air. As I watched her ladycock flutter in spasms, I pressed my cunt forward as far as I could to press the big dildo against the back wall of my cavern. As it continued to pound in and out of me, I clamped down hard over the phallus and groaned out another long hard climax. Velvet watched me twist and jerk in my harness, her big chili pepper twitching and jerking as if applause of my accomplishment.

Suddenly, she reached down beside her chair and stood up holding a strap-on dildo. She quickly fastened it around her waist, then inserted her throbbing clit in the hollow end of the tube, then she turned off the fucking machine and yanked on the floor handle to ratchet me up to her height. Then, without warning, she thrust her big dildo inside me and began fucking me wildly. I was still coming down from last orgasm but the sight of her fucking me with the strap-on dildo quickly resurfaced the tingling between my legs and I soon felt another orgasm beginning to well up within me.

"Yes, Velvet," I screamed. "Fuck me harder. Make me come again, master. It feels good."

Velvet's eyes opened wide and she peered deeply into my eyes, looking at me like a wild animal. The hollow dildo was obviously providing some kind of direct friction for her also, and I could tell from her panting and hip action that she was on the verge with me.

"I'm going to cum again, master," I said. "Cum inside my hot cunt. Fuck me!"

Velvet grabbed the side of my harness and suddenly pulled me tight against her body as she pushed forward in one final powerful thrust.

"Uhnnn," she groaned, as I sprayed one last long stream of love juices all over her bare lips and asshole.

When we both finally stopping cumming, Velvet pulled out of me and watched me swinging helplessly above the slippery floor. For the first time in almost two hours, I felt all the tension and stress of being bound and suspended in thin air slip away. I'd become fully satisfied being her submissive slave.

VOLUME TWO

THE SLAVE

1

I always looked forward to my weekly lunch date with my best friend and professional sex therapist, Hannah. But today, I had a different reason for wanting to see her. My sex life had become a bit staid and boring lately, and I wanted some new ideas for how to spice things up. As a newly liberated, polysexual woman, I'd had plenty of variety in my relationships, but I was tired of being the one always taking the lead seeking out new adventures. I wanted someone *else* to be in charge of plotting my sexual journey for a change.

I smiled when I saw Hannah waiting in the foyer of the trendy new Chicago restaurant, *Girl & the Goat*. Besides being my best friend and a font of sexual knowledge, she was super-hot, and my pussy tingled remembering our last tryst in the bushes behind the public library.

"Funny you chose *this* place for our meet-up this week," I said, kissing her gently on the cheek.

"How so?" she said. "I thought you'd like it, with its vegan menu and convenient location next to the 'el'.

"No, it's not that. It's the name: Girl & the Goat. Given your profession and everything, it sounds like some kind of weird kink."

"Ha," Hannah chuckled. "It's certainly provocative, but I suspect it has more to do with the executive chef being a woman, and her proclivity toward farm-to-table food."

"Either way," I said, licking my lips. "As long as *you're* somewhere in the mix, I'm sure it will be super tasty."

After we sat down and ordered our entrees and some cocktails, Hannah rested her elbows on the table and leaned over toward me.

"What's up, girl?" she said, scrunching her eyebrows in concern. "You sounded a little down-in-the-dumps when I chatted with you last time over the phone."

"I dunno," I said. "I just feel like I'm in a bit of a rut. You know, *relationship*-wise."

"Are we talking about your *love* life or your *sex* life?" she said, smiling toward the waiter as he placed our drinks on the table.

"You know me," I laughed, taking a healthy swig of my margarita. "I'm still not ready for another long-term relationship after my last failed marriage. My sex life just feels kind of–predictable–lately."

Hannah suddenly hunched forward, coughing as she took a sip of her cosmopolitan.

"*Predictable?*" she said. "This coming from the girl who just came off a fling with the First Lady of the United States?!"

"That was a little different, I grant you. It's just that in most of my recent relationships, *I've* been the one taking the lead. I'm kind of getting tired having to take the first step and always being the one in charge in the bedroom department. Sometimes a girl just wants to be a lady, you know what I mean?"

"You mean being the *submissive* one for a change?" she said.

"I guess so. *You're* the sex therapist. Does there always have to be a top and a bottom, for want of a better expression, in every sexual relationship?"

Hannah paused while the waiter returned with our entrees, placing them in front of us on our place settings.

"That's the age-old question," she said, picking up one of her goat-cheese empanadas and chomping into it. "Traditionally, there's always been one dom and one submissive is most pair-bonds. I think it's a natural outgrowth of the old hunter-gatherer role of the male in a traditional heterosexual relationship and the homemaker/child-rearing role of the woman."

"Haven't we outgrown those old stereotypes in this modern enlightened age?" I said, shaking my head.

"You'd think so. But it seems to run deeper than that. Maybe it's a more visceral impulse, like with the alpha-beta-omega dynamic in a wolf pack. Whether they're hetero, gay, or lesbian, most couples naturally seem to assume one role or the other. With gays, it takes the form of 'tops' and 'bottoms' and with lesbians there's usually a 'butch' and a 'femme.'"

"But aren't these roles becoming more *fluid* these days with couples swapping positions from time to time?"

"Yes, of course," Hannah said, washing down her empanada with another gulp of her cosmo. "But each person seems to revert back eventually to their preferred position in the hierarchy. This seems like an odd question coming from such a sexually liberated person like yourself. It seems like you've tried just about *everything*. In fact, if I remember correctly, didn't you once avail yourself of the services of a professional dominatrix? Did you enjoy playing the submissive role in that situation?"

"Yes, but it all felt so manufactured, and temporary. Like I was *paying* to be dominated. It didn't feel natural."

Hannah shrugged her shoulders and chuckled.

"Well, you could pretty much walk into any lesbian bar in this town and find a dominant butch to take you on for a longer-term ride. With your pretty looks and that sexy body, you'd have no trouble picking up someone who's looking for some girly-girl fun."

"Mm, I don't know," I said, scrunching up my nose. "I'm not really attracted to that kind of woman. I guess I'm just looking for a 'normal' girl who I could experiment playing a more submissive role."

"What did you have in mind exactly?" Hannah said, leaning back in her chair.

"I don't know, someone pretty, kind of like *you*, who's not afraid to take the lead for a while..."

"Just how far did you want to take this whole submissive thing?"
she said, arching an eyebrow.

"Whatever," I said, nibbling on one of my chickpea fritters. "I
could go all-in, for a little while at least. It might be kind of fun,
letting my partner have her way with me for a change."

"Hmm," Hannah purred, as a sly smile began to spread across her
lips.

"*What?*" I said. "What are you thinking all of a sudden?"

"It's been a while since the two of us have had a roll in the hay, so
to speak. Why don't we mix it up a little this time? I'll play the domme
and you can be the submissive."

"That sounds like fun," I nodded, feeling my panties moistening at
the thought of reconnecting with Hannah sexually. "But we've both
had plenty of turns being the one on top–"

"No," she said. "I mean in a more *formal* type of domme and
submissive role."

"You mean like in a BDSM type of thing?"

"Kind of," she smiled. "I was thinking more in terms of a *master-
and-slave* type of role."

I lifted my hand to my mouth, suddenly coughing on a chick pea.
Now it was *my* turn to be surprised.

"You want me to be your *slave*?" I said. "What would that entail,
exactly?"

"Whatever I deem necessary," she smirked. "Whatever I want you
to do, *whenever* and *wherever* we might find ourselves."

"You mean like in public places too?"

"Yes," Hannah nodded. "If the mood strikes me."

"That sounds kind of fun," I said, suddenly squirming in my chair
at the thought of being at Hannah's behest whenever she demanded.
"When did you want to start this little experiment?"

"How about right *now*?" Hannah said, peering at me with a
devilish grin.

2

"Okay..." I said, suddenly intrigued. "What did you have in mind exactly?"

"I want you to get under the table and eat my pussy."

"Right *here*? Right *now*? There must be a hundred people in this place, and we're only separated by a few feet!"

Hannah peered at me as a slight curl formed in the corner of her lip.

"I'm going to get up and create a distraction. When you see the right opportunity, duck under the table. Nobody should notice with everything else that's going on. And the long table covering should disguise you while you're under there."

"What about when I need to get *out*?" I said, wrinkling my forehead in dismay.

"We'll figure that out when the time comes," Hannah said. "Now get ready. You won't have much time to make your move when the opportunity presents."

"Are you sure this is a good idea–" I said, peering around me at all the restaurant patrons talking amongst themselves mere inches away from us.

"Don't worry your pretty little head about it," she said, rising from her chair. "This shouldn't take long. I'll be back in a flash."

Hannah picked up her purse and began walking toward the restaurant washroom. As she approached a waiter carrying a tray of food on his shoulder, she peered down into her purse, pretending to look for something. Suddenly, she tripped toward the waiter, and he stumbled, dropping the tray of food and beverages onto the floor with a noisy clatter.

"Oh my God!" Hannah cried, pretending to be just as surprised as the shaken waiter. "I'm so sorry. I was just looking for something in my purse–"

"Not to worry," the waiter said, bending down to pick up the fallen dishes and broken glasses on the floor. "These things happen more often than you can imagine around here. Are you alright? Did I spill anything on you?"

While the two of them continued their discussion, I glanced around me, and noticing that all eyes had turned temporarily toward the distraction on the other side of the restaurant, I flipped up the table covering and ducked underneath, feeling my heart pounding like a freight train.

I could hear Hannah and the waiter talking in the distance, then things slowly quieted down as the normal hum of chatter of the lunch guests talking and the kitchen staff working resumed. After a few minutes, Hannah returned to the table, placing her purse on the floor beside her and sitting down quietly in her chair. Fortunately for both of us, she'd chosen to wear a mid-length skirt today that provided ready access to her lower region while providing a modicum of cover from the surrounding restaurant guests.

Hannah slowly spread her legs apart and I could see in the dim light under the table a small wet spot in the middle of her sheer panties. Smiling at the ingenuity of her brilliant ruse, I reached under her skirt and threaded my thumbs under the top of her panties, slowly pulling them down to her ankles. I could see her bald pussy glistening from the moisture that had accumulated on her tumescent labia, and I paused for a moment admiring her pretty vulva.

"Ahem," Hannah coughed above me, strumming her fingers impatiently on the table.

Taking her cue to proceed, I spread her legs further apart and pressed my face between the gap, slowly licking the inside of her quivering thighs. Although I was nominally the submissive one in this unusual situation, that didn't mean I couldn't tease her for a bit and enjoy a certain degree of control while I followed her bidding.

As I moved my face closer to her steaming pussy, she shifted her hips forward, pressing her pubis toward my mouth. When I felt her wet slit touch my lips, I extended my tongue and slid it gently between her folds. Hannah groaned softly as she scrunched down lower in her chair, and I moved my hands under her skirt to grab the sides of her cheeks, pulling her harder into my face. As she slowly began to undulate her hips against my face, I raised my head, drawing a line upward between her dripping slit toward her exposed bulb. I could see it peeking out of its hood now, like a ripe cherry dangling on a tree.

Hannah flapped her thighs in and out around the sides of my head, and I could tell she was growing impatient for me to take her into my mouth. Realizing that we'd have a limited amount of time to consummate this act, I open my lips and sucked her gland into my mouth, rolling my tongue over her hardened shaft.

Hannah lurched forward and moaned as the dinnerware shook on the table above me. Feeling newly empowered by tormenting her while the rest of the restaurant patrons went about their business oblivious to what was happening mere inches away, I snaked my right hand up between her thighs and thrust two fingers into her tight hole. She gripped the sides of the table with her two hands, trying to maintain her composure in the packed lunchroom. Suddenly, I heard some footsteps approach our table and the sound of our waiter's voice talking to Hannah.

"I see that you've finished your main course," he said. "Would you like something for dessert?"

Hannah peered up at him with glazed eyes.

"Oh, um—sure," she said, clamping my face between her legs

trying to stop me from what I was doing while she spoke to the waiter.

"What do you have on offer?" she said, too distracted to look at the menu.

"Today's special is French silk pie or our signature Girl & the Goat cupcakes."

"The cupcakes sound fine, thank you," Hannah said.

"And for your *friend*?" the waiter said, peering at my half-finished plate of fritters. "Will she be rejoining you soon?"

I smiled as I listened to Hannah pretend like everything was normal while I continued curling my fingers inside her throbbing pussy toward her G-spot. She coughed as she jerked in her chair, trying to suppress the pleasure that was rapidly consuming her body.

"She just had to freshen up in the washroom," she said to the waiter. "I'm sure she'll join us again shortly. We'll order her dessert when she returns."

"As you wish," the waiter said. "I'll be back in a few minutes."

"Thank you," Hannah squeaked, her voice suddenly breaking from the feeling of my hands and fingers caressing her under the table.

When the waiter left, Hannah spread her legs further apart and she reached under the table, pulling my head toward her pussy firmly with one hand.

"You better get this over with fast," she whispered. "Before the waiter comes back and begins to wonder what happened to you. Besides, you're driving me crazy. I need to get off soon or I'll never be able to finish my meal."

Feeling just as eager to bring her to climax in full view of the other restaurant patrons, I stepped up the pace of my licking and sucking, drawing her button hard into my mouth.

"Yes, baby," Hannah purred. "Suck my pussy. I'm going to come in your mouth with everybody watching. You're being such a good little slave."

Hannah's dirty talk was turning me on almost as much as it must have been for her, and I squeezed her ass tightly imagining what it must have felt like to have someone licking your pussy surrounded by so many people. Her hips began to shake and I could hear her panting more rapidly above me over the table. I pushed my fingers harder up inside her, pressing my knuckles hard against her dripping slit while I flicked my tongue over her clit and curled my fingers against her G-spot.

Suddenly, Hannah grabbed the sides of my head with two hands and pulled my face tightly against her splayed legs as her hips buckled against my head. I could hear her groaning softly above me while she tried to suppress the waves of pleasure rolling over her as her pussy clamped down over my fingers in a series of powerful contractions. I held her nub in my mouth, feeling the walls of her pussy contracting around my fingers until her hips stopped quivering and her buttock muscles slowly relaxed. After giving her a moment to recover from her orgasm, I pulled my fingers out of her pussy and sat back on the heels of my feet under the table.

"What *now*?" I whispered to her through the draped tablecloth. "How am I going to get out of here now?"

"I don't know," Hannah said. "I don't think I can get away with another waiter distraction. Maybe you can just roll out of there pretending like you dropped something."

Hannah reached into her purse and tossed her compact onto the floor beside me. I picked it up and hesitated for a moment, then I flung the side of the tablecloth aside and rolled out from under the table, trying to appear as nonchalant as possible.

"I knew I'd dropped this thing *somewhere*," I said, holding up the compact to the startled guests sitting next to our table, then sitting down on my chair like nothing unusual had happened.

"Well *that* was invigorating," I said, smiling at Hannah as the lunch guests resumed their usual discourse.

"I'll say," she said, reaching down to pull up her panties. "I practically burst a gasket when the waiter came by at the worst possible moment. You weren't very helpful when you didn't take my cue to stop stimulating me while I pressed my thighs against your head."

"Oh *come on*," I said, smiling at her with a fiendish grin. "I couldn't let *you* be the only one having all the fun."

"Maybe so," she grinned, her face still flushed from the after-effects of her recent climax. "But it looks like I'm going to have to teach you a little more discipline about what it means to be a proper sex slave."

"Oh?" I said, raising a playful eyebrow. "What did you have in mind next for me?"

"You're going to have to wait until we finish our meal," she said, noticing the waiter approaching our table once again.

"Here are your cupcakes, ma'am," he said, placing a dish with two cupcakes on the placemat in front of her. Then he turned toward me, nodding toward my unfinished main course. "Were you finished with your entree, ma'am? Perhaps you'd like something for desert also?"

I paused for a moment, peering over at Hannah playfully while I glanced down at her plate.

"I'll have whatever *she's* having," I said, picking up one of her cupcakes and mashing it into my mouth as the icing dripped around the edges of my mouth.

3

———

After lunch, Hannah drove me back to her place, but she wouldn't tell me what she had in store for me next. When we pulled into her driveway, she led me out of the car and up her stairs into her master bathroom. Without saying a word, she turned on the large glass-enclosed shower and began to undress me. As the room began to fill with the warm mist from the running water, I looked over at her with a puzzled expression.

"What are you planning to do with me now?" I said. "Give me a golden shower?"

"That wasn't my intent," she said. "But now that you mention it, that's not a bad idea. No, I have some *other* dirty ideas in mind for you. But first I need to get us cleaned up in preparation for the next step in your education as a slave."

"Mmm, I like the sound of that," I smiled. "Are you coming in the shower with me?"

"Mm, hmm," Hannah nodded. "But don't get too excited. This is all about attending to *my* needs, not the other way around."

"That's okay," I said. "Just being in the shower naked with you will satisfy my needs for the rest of the day."

After Hannah removed the rest of my clothes, she disrobed and the two of us stepped into the warm spray of the shower.

"Mmm, this is delightful," I said, sliding my naked body against hers as the water began to coat our slippery bodies.

"The first rule about being a slave is no *touching* unless otherwise instructed," she said, pushing me away. "Now pick up the bar of soap and give me a proper cleansing, and I mean *everywhere.*"

"Okay..." I said, picking up the jasmine-scented bar of soap from the soap dish and beginning to rub it over Hannah's shoulders and tits.

"That's a good slave," she purred. "I want you to rub every square inch of me—and don't forget all the hidden crevasses."

"It'll be my pleasure," I said, ogling Hannah's glistening body under the bright light of the shower.

As instructed, I was careful to roll the soap over every part of her body, starting at the top and working my way downward. When I reached her mound, I felt the bar of soap sticking for a moment on the short stubble of her pubis, and the bar fell onto the floor.

"Sorry, Hannah," I said, bending down to retrieve the bar.

"That's okay," she said, peering at my upturned butt as I leaned over at the waist. "I kind of prefer you from this angle anyway. But from now on, I want you to refer to me as Master. I will refer to you simply as Slave."

Hannah slapped my ass hard from behind and I lurched forward, almost losing my footing on the slippery floor. Then she reached between my legs and clamped her hand around my upturned mound with a firm grip, pulling me toward her.

"Do you *like* it when I play rough with you, Slave?"

Mmm, yes, Master," I sputtered as the water streamed down my back and flowed over the front of my face.

Hannah slapped my other butt cheek hard before instructing me to resume my cleaning ritual.

"Now stand up and finish the job. You still haven't finished cleaning my lower regions."

"Yes, Master," I said, repositioning myself in front of her and rolling the bar of soap over her mound and between her legs toward her perineum.

"Yes," Hannah jerked, feeling the slippery bar sliding over her sensitive parts. "Just like that. I want you to give my private parts extra special attention."

"Yes, Master," I smiled, angling the bar between her folds and rubbing it softly over the base of her mound where her clit poked out, aroused by the combination of the slippery soap rubbing against her and the warm water streaming between her legs.

But just as I was getting into lavishing her pussy with the slippery bar, she turned around and tilted her ass up with her hands resting on the side of the shower wall.

"Now clean my pucker too," she instructed. "I want to feel you caressing *every* part of me."

"Mmm," I hummed, only too happy to touch the most private parts of her body.

I separated her butt cheeks, then slowly ran the bar of soap between her crack, caressing her rosebud with the tips of my fingers.

"Yes," she panted. "I like the touch of your fingers on my butthole. Now coat your fingers with some soap and insert two of them inside me."

"In your *anus*?" I said, shocked at the audacity of her invitation.

"Yes," she said. "Just a little way, up to the first knuckle or so. I want to see what it feels like to have you rim me with your fingers."

I rolled the bar of soap in my hands then pressed my forefinger and middle finger slowly into her sphincter, being careful to keep my nails pointed upward so as not to pinch her sensitive tissue.

"*Fuck* yes," Hannah hissed, pressing her ass back toward me to meet the pressure of my probing fingers. "Now curl them around in there a little bit like when you finger my pussy."

As I began to gently move my fingers around in her butthole, I was surprised how much of a turn-on it was for me. This was something I'd never really explored before, and there was something very sexy and raunchy about pegging my girlfriend from behind, even if it *was* just with the tips of my fingers. Her sphincter was tighter than I imagined, and I felt my pussy throbbing under the warm flow of water splashing over the two of us while I probed her from behind.

"That's enough," she suddenly said, tilting her hips forward and making a plopping sound as my fingers popped out of her hole. "Now wash your hands with the bar of soap and rinse the rest of my perineum before cleaning my legs and feet."

While I followed Hannah's instructions, I slowly bent down at my knees, moving further and further down her body until I reached her feet. She lifted up one foot then the other, giving me access to the bottom of her soles, then she grabbed my wet hair, pulling my face hard into her open pussy. I choked for a moment from the combined pressure of her wet flesh covering my nose and mouth and from the cascade of water pouring down over her stomach onto my upturned face. But instead of giving me a chance to continue licking and sucking her pussy as in the restaurant, after a few seconds she pulled my head back and peered down at me while I blinked up at her under the spray of falling water.

"That's a good slave," she smiled. "I think we're finished in here. Now get up and fetch me a towel to dry me off."

"Yes, Master," I said, disappointed that she wasn't going to give me a chance to finish the job I'd started.

I scrambled out of the shower and tip-toed over the wet floor to retrieve a bath towel from the towel rack, then Hannah stepped out of the shower and turned around while I patted her dry.

"That'll do," Hannah said, taking the towel from me and walking over to the padded stool in front of her make-up mirror. "Now I want you to attend to some personal grooming. Get on your knees on the floor while I gather the necessary tools."

What kind of tools did she have in mind? I thought. *She's really getting into this whole role-playing scenario.*

But it didn't bother me since I was actually enjoying this little role reversal and eager to see what she had in mind next. I bent down on the wet tile floor, wondering why she hadn't allowed me to towel myself dry, feeling the residual water from the shower dripping out of my hair down the middle of my back and over the crack of my ass. I shivered from the sensation, not because I was cold, but from the feeling of the warm water caressing my splayed labia and tingling clit, now fully exposed from my heightened state of arousal.

When Hannah returned, she placed a women's razor and a tube of shave gel on the floor beside me, then she sat down on the stool, spreading her legs wide in front of my face.

"It's been a while since I've shaved my pussy," she said. "It's getting a little rough down there. I want you to shave me nice and smooth, just like you are."

Hannah knew that I'd undergone laser treatment to remove every trace of hair from my perineum area, but she'd been holding off having similar treatment for fear of the pain involved in the procedure.

"And you better be careful not to cut or nick me down there, or there'll be severe consequences."

"Yes ma'am–er, *Master*," I said, squeezing a dollop of gel onto my hands and rubbing it gently over her scruffy mound and stubbly labia.

It took me a good thirty minutes to finish shaving her, especially the super-sensitive area on the sides of her vulva and along her perineum between her pussy and her asshole. Although I was nervous about cutting her at various times, the act of shaving her most private regions with a sharp blade while I stared at her dripping pussy was a tremendous turn on. I could feel my own juices running down the insides of my thighs while I smiled at Hannah's inflamed clit and tumescent lips as I carefully trimmed her stubble.

When I finished, she picked up a hand-held mirror from the vanity table and angled it toward her snatch, admiring my handiwork.

"You did a good job, Slave," she smiled, rubbing her hand over her smooth-as-velvet skin. "There might be a little reward in this for you later if you continue to be a good girl. But first, there's one other grooming job I want you to attend to while you're down there."

Hannah fetched another bag of items from one of the drawers, then unzipped the bag and handed me a nail file.

"I haven't done my *nails* in a while either," she said. "I want you to file them down a quarter of an inch and make them just as smooth as my pussy."

I took one look at the length of her nails and furrowed my forehead.

"Have you got some clippers? It's going to take quite a while to sand them down that much–"

Hannah grabbed my wet hair and pulled my face up to meet her angry gaze.

"Remember who's in *charge* here," Hannah said. "I want you to take your time and do them the professional way. And don't talk back to your master like that. You've got to learn your position as my slave. Now get to work."

As I lifted one of Hannah's feet and began sanding her toenails with the nail file, I began to wonder if this whole dom and submissive thing was still a good idea. She seemed to be getting a little too seriously into the role. She was no longer the happy-go-lucky, always-joking-around best friend I remembered. I figured I'd entertain her with this little escapade for another couple of hours or so. Then I'd be happy to revert back to my usual role taking the lead in my sexual affairs.

But as I looked up at Hannah with doleful eyes, she peered down and winked at me with a lopsided smile.

I guess she's just getting into character, I thought. *Let's see how far she wants to take this thing. Maybe she's trying to teach me a lesson.*

As I caressed her soft feet, I glanced up at her newly shaven pussy and noticed a dribble of lubrication dripping out of her hole and down the crack of her ass. I peered back up at her and winked with my opposite eye.

Yin and Yang. Tops and bottoms. Domme and femme. Maybe this was the natural way of the world after all.

4

After I finished Hannah's pedicure, she leaned over and towel-dried my hair then patted me down to remove the last vestiges of water remaining on my back. Then she held out her hand and raised me off my knees, leading me toward the bedroom. When we got to her large four-poster bed, we stopped and I looked at her expectantly, hoping we'd finally have a chance to connect and have sex like we used to. Instead, she just looked at me blankly then pushed me backwards over the foot of the bed, where I toppled onto her mattress face up with my legs spread apart.

"Perfect," she said. "Stay in that position while I collect a few things for our next act."

Hannah fished through her chest of drawers, then returned with a jumble of scarves, placing them on the bed beside me.

"Mmm," I said, smiling at her with a raised eyebrow. "Are you going to blindfold me?"

"No," she said. "But you won't be needing your eyes for this next thing I have in mind. Or your *hands*, for that matter."

Hannah picked up one of the scarves and wound it around my right wrist, then she pulled my arm up to the corner of the bed near the headboard and tied the loose ends around one of the posts, double-tying the knot firmly. Then she went around to the other side of the bed and repeated the procedure, tying my other hand to the other post. As she walked down toward the foot of the bed, she looked at me with a sly smile then she grasped my two feet and pulled me forcefully toward her, stretching my arms out straight.

"Ow!" I said, more playfully than actually hurting in pain. "There's no need to be so rough with me."

"I'm sorry if I hurt your feelings," Hannah smirked. "Remember, this whole thing was *your* idea. You can stop it at any time you want by saying the magic word."

"You mean 'stop', or 'I don't want to play anymore'?"

"Either of those will do. You're always in charge of what happens to your body."

I peered up at her with a little girl pout, then smiled.

"No," I said. "I don't want you to stop. I just want you to remember who you're playing with here. Someday the tables might be turned around the other way."

"Oh, I *definitely* know what I'm playing with," Hannah said as she tied my two feet to the bottom bedposts, admiring my naked body spread-eagled on top of her mattress. "And I plan to take maximum advantage of it while I have the chance."

She crawled up onto the mattress from the base of the bed and kneeled between my legs, running her eyes up and down my figure.

"You look absolutely delectable in this position, Jade," she said, her eyes widening at the prospect of ravishing me in my helpless state. "I'm going to take my time getting off this time while you caress and nibble every part of my body."

"That might be kind of hard to do in my current predicament," I said, thrashing my hands and feet to remind her of my limited mobility.

"That's okay," she said. "You're not going to need any of those extra appendages with what I'm planning to do to you. Everything except your *mouth*, that is. I have special plans for *that* part of your anatomy."

"Mmm," I purred, happy to have a chance to lick her body again.

"Well then, scooch right on up here. I'll be happy to eat your pussy while you sit on my face–"

"All in good time, my dear," she said. "But first, there's a few *other* parts of your body I'd like to play with."

Hannah lifted one of her knees and straddled my left thigh, then lowered her pussy on top of my warm skin. I could feel her wetness coating my leg as she began to rock her hips against my flexing upper thigh muscle.

"Your skin feels so soft, Jade," she said, temporarily dispensing with the pejorative term she'd used for me previously. "You've done a nice job shaving my peachka nice and smooth. You feel exquisite against my skin."

"As do you, Han–I mean *Master*," I said. "I can feel your juices coating my leg."

"Yes," Hannah nodded. "I plan on leaving my mark all over you before I'm finished with you."

"Fuck, yes," I said, lifting my hips off the mattress, begging her to move her body closer to my aching snatch.

Hannah looked down at my bald pussy and licked her lips. Then she slowly dragged her dripping crotch over the length of my upper thigh, pausing when she reaching my apex. I could feel the warmth of her left thigh pressing up against my vulva, and I humped my hips, vainly trying to gain the necessary friction to stimulate my clit.

Noticing the desperation in my eyes, she lifted herself off me temporarily, then repositioned herself straddling my upper pelvis with her two legs. Then she lowered her wet pussy onto the top of my mound and proceeded to grind her clit against my hard pubic bone. She let out a deep guttural moan and I tried to angle my hips upward to gain traction on my own burning gland, but instead she pressed me back down onto the mattress, careful to position her pussy just out of reach of my tingling gland.

"You're *evil*, you know that?" I hissed, giving her a death stare.

"It's all part of the role, baby," she smiled. "You wanted to be the slave. It's your job to give *me* pleasure, not the other way around."

"*Fine*," I huffed. "I'm enjoying the show plenty enough as it is. In fact, I could probably get off just watching you rub your pussy against my muff."

"I suppose you could," Hannah said, knowing full well as a sex therapist about neurological phenomenon of referred pleasure and pain. "I guess we'll just have to find another way to stimulate my pussy then."

Hannah wiggled her body up higher on my torso, shifting her weight from one knee to the other until she reached my tits, which by now were swollen and distended from the intense stimulation I was experiencing. Then she lowered her dripping pussy onto one of my erect teats and proceeded to fuck my little phallus between her slippery labia.

"Oh my God," I hummed. "That feels incredible. Fuck my tit with your pretty pussy, Hannah."

"*Who?*" she said, glaring at me indignantly.

"I mean *Master*. Fuck me with your smooth pussy, Master. I want to watch you cum all over my big tits."

"I'd love to accommodate you, my dear," she smiled. "But I have other plans for cumming all over you."

She suddenly lifted herself up and turned her body around with her ass toward my head then slowly inched her gaping hole up toward my face.

"Yes," I panted. "Sit on my face. I want to suck on that nicely shaved pussy and flick my tongue all over that big bean."

"I think we can manage that," Hannah said, lowering her glistening crotch onto my eagerly awaiting mouth.

When I felt her slippery folds press against my face, I lapped up her juices like a hungry puppy dog. She pressed her pelvis hard against my jaw, and I could feel her hard button rubbing against the top row of my teeth. I spread my lips to give her maximum friction against the hard surface, and she began to rock her hips rapidly forward and back. The crack of her ass kept rubbing against my nose, but this only added to the excitement of the situation, especially as I inhaled the sweet smell of the jasmine still lingering on her skin.

While Hannah picked up the pace of her rocking and grinding, she bent forward and began licking my tits, wildly rimming my tingling nipples with her slathering tongue. As I watched her pretty pucker flexing inches away from my wide eyes, I began to feel the familiar pangs of an orgasm building up inside me. But once again, just as I was about to reach the crest of my pleasure, she lifted herself off me, holding her body inches away from my flapping tongue desperately trying to reach her inflamed clit.

"What the fuck, Hannah–" I started to object.

But I didn't have a chance to finish my complaint as she tilted her hips forward, planting her ass directly over my lips.

"Shut up and lick my asshole, Slave," she huffed. "There's plenty of *other* ways we can put that talented tongue to work."

At first, I was surprised by the temerity of Hannah's bold move, but as she began to spread her legs further apart and wiggle her ass on my face, I quickly forgot about what part of her body I was licking and began munching on her anus with unremitted abandon. There was no trace of any unpleasant smell or taste, only the warm feeling of her soft flesh in my mouth and the sweet smell of the jasmine body wash.

As Hannah began to moan in delight above me, I extended my tongue and probed her hole, rolling it around the edges and washing it with my warm saliva. I'd never licked a woman's asshole before, but I knew that it was a highly erogenous zone and that it was everyone's fantasy. And from the sound of Hannah's rapidly escalating whimpers and moans above me, it was obvious this was one of *Hannah's* too.

As she began to shake her hips more rapidly over my face and press her weight down harder onto my face, I could see her butt cheeks beginning to quiver in a state of imminent climax. When her orgasm finally hit her, Hannah wailed at the top of her lungs as her whole body shook like she was having an epileptic seizure. When I felt her sphincter pulsing in my mouth, I couldn't hold back any longer and I raised my hips high off the mattress, gushing like a faucet from my own powerful orgasm taking hold of me. For what seemed like an eternity, the two of us swiveled our hips wildly, locked in the most powerful orgasm either one of us had experienced in a long time.

Referred pleasure indeed, I thought as my orgasm slowly began to ebb. *Maybe I should try this role-play stuff more often.*

5

———————

When Hannah finally stopped shaking over top of my face, she lifted herself up and flopped down on the mattress beside me, breathing heavily.

"Holy *fuck*," I said. "Was that just me, or was that the most erotic, powerful orgasm I've had in a long time?"

"No," she panted. "You aren't kidding. I haven't cum that hard, since, well, the *last* time I was with you."

"Who knew the anus could be such a pleasure receptor?" I said, licking my tongue over my mouth to taste the remnants of her scent still on my lips.

"I guess the gay guys are on to something after all," she nodded.

I turned my head toward her and peered at her with a sly smile.

"That's the *real* reason you wanted me to wash you down there, isn't it? You had this whole thing planned right from the beginning."

"Maybe, she smirked. But the pussy shave and pedicure also helped to put me in the mood. I almost came watching you stare at my pussy while you filed my nails."

"You're such a bitch," I said, giving her a gentle nudge with my elbow.

"That's bitch-*Master*, to you," she grinned back at me.

"Yes Master," I nodded obsequiously. "So what now? Are you going to untie me and let me properly satisfy myself now? If I don't touch my clit soon, I'm going to explode."

"Maybe in a little while," Hannah said, giving me a devilish smile. "There's one last thing I wanted to do to you before we end this little submissive and dom thing."

"I can't imagine what else you could do to me that could be more defiling than rubbing your asshole into my face while I'm helplessly tied up."

"Oh, you have *no* idea," she said, getting up off the bed and heading back to her chest of drawers, where she retrieved a huge pink strap-on dildo.

"No *way*!" I said, shaking my head. "You weren't thinking of fucking me up the *ass* with that thing!?"

"Probably not," she smirked. "But I *do* like the idea of fucking you from behind with it."

Hannah placed the dildo on the bed and slowly untied each of my hands from the bedposts. Then she flipped me over and retied my hands in the same position, this time with me facing down onto the mattress.

"Holy shit, Hannah," I said. "Now I'm even more vulnerable than before. You can pretty much do whatever you want to me in this position."

"That's exactly the idea," she said, slowly strapping on the silicon dildo like she was a cowboy preparing for a gunslinging contest.

"Be careful with that thing," I said as she approached the side of the bed, estimating the length of the phallus at a good eight inches. "You could take someone's eye out with that thing if you're not too careful."

"Oh, don't worry," Hannah smiled. "I don't plan on going anywhere near your *face* with my pretty little cock. I've got some other plans for it. Now I'm *really* going to show you what it means to be a dom and a submissive."

Hannah hopped up on the bed straddling my hips and positioned her crotch directly above my bare ass cheeks. Then she rocked her hips up and down overtop of me, causing the flexible appendage attached to her harness to slap loudly against my buttocks.

"You said you wanted something to touch your pussy," she said. "Well get ready, because you're about to have the ride of your life."

"Yes, Master," I whinnied, tilting my ass up as much as my restraints allowed to give her freer access to my pussy.

For a long moment, Hannah paused inches above my ass with her weapon, and for a second I thought she was contemplating fucking me up the ass with it. But when I felt her grab the end of the dildo and swipe it gently up and down my quivering slit, I moaned in anticipation of her filling my aching cunt.

"Fuck me with your big dick, Master," I pleaded. "I need you to fill me up with your organ. I want to feel you inside me."

"Oh yes," Hannah grunted, positioning the tip of the phallus at the entrance to my dripping hole.

She pushed it in an inch or two, then paused for a moment before plunging it all the way inside my tight snatch.

"Uhn!" I grunted, feeling the probe pressing against the end of my cavity.

"Oh *God*, Hannah," I said, momentarily dispensing with the proper terms I was supposed to use in our little game of top and bottom. "Fuck me with that thing like there's no tomorrow."

"Damn *straight*, girl," Hannah hissed, equally lost in the moment.

As she lowered her body onto my back, I felt her cool tits rubbing against my shoulder blades while she began to pound her hips forcefully against my buttocks. With each thrust, I clenched my cheeks, reveling in the feeling of her hard mound pressing up against me. She was fucking me hard and deep enough that I could feel the base of the dildo ramming against my tingling clit, and I tilted my hips up a degree or two higher to generate more friction.

It didn't take long for the feelings of another powerful orgasm to well up inside me, and as we both slapped our hips together like two bucking broncos, our combined cries of ecstasy escalated in likewise fashion. At the crest of my pleasure, I cried out to Hannah to signal that I was about to come.

"I'm going to cum, Han. I'm going to cum hard all over your big cock. Ram that monster inside me while I gush all over you pussy."

"*Fuck* yes," Hannah grunted, pressing her hips hard against my ass in one final forceful thrust as her tits quivered against my back at the beginning of another strong orgasm.

When I felt her cumming on top of me, I couldn't hold back and longer and I screamed at the top of my lungs as my entire vulva began flexing and clamping in a series of powerful contractions while the built-up fluid inside my pussy began spraying out the sides of our tight connection all over Hannah's buckling thighs behind the leather of her strap-on harness.

When we both finally stopped cumming after waking up the entire neighborhood, Hannah collapsed on top of my back with the dildo still inserted deep inside me, resting her head softly against my throbbing heart. Even though she had me in the most compromised possible submissive and dominant position possible at this moment, I could feel the love and tenderness emanating from her body as she wrapped her arms tenderly around me, softly caressing the sides of my breasts.

6

Hannah pulled the dildo out of me, then we cuddled for a while and fell asleep atop her mattress for a couple of hours. When I woke up, I heard her foraging around in the kitchen and I went downstairs to see what she was up to. When I saw that she was preparing a pasta salad, I peered up at her with a quizzical expression.

"I thought your *slave* was supposed to do all the domestic work," I joked. "Shouldn't *I* be the one getting dinner ready?"

She turned toward me and smiled.

"I thought maybe you'd like to switch roles for a while," she said. "Aren't you growing tired of being the submissive one yet?"

"Not really," I said with a sheepish grin. "After that last experience, I'm kind of getting into it. It's kind of fun being the bottom for a change."

"Just how far do you want to go with this thing?" she said, spooning some of the salad into a bowl and sliding it across the kitchen island toward me.

"*You're* the one in charge here," I said. "Use your imagination. Surely there must be a few *other* ways you can think of to use and abuse me."

Hannah pulled up a chair beside me and sat down to eat her salad as her eyes flitted around trying to think of what to do next. After a few minutes, she peered up at me with a mischievous smile on her face.

"*What?*" I said. "What are you dreaming up now?"

"It seems to me that the obvious next step in your evolution as a slave is to test the waters with a few *other* players. How would you feel about my taking you to a lesbian bar?"

"That doesn't sound like too much of a stretch," I said. "It's not like I haven't picked up a girl in a bar before..."

"Not the kind of bar *I* have in mind. It's pretty hard-core. Plus, I have an idea how we could make it a little more interesting."

"Oh?" I said. "Do tell."

"I was thinking maybe we could dress you up in a provocative costume, something more befitting of your role as a slave. Then we could *really* test how strong this dominant-submissive impulse is in a natural setting."

"What, you mean like in some kind of tight leather outfit or something?"

"Something like that," Hannah smiled. "Why don't we go to our friend Cheryl's sex shop and try a few things on? She's got some pretty wild outfits in the back."

"Okay," I said, feeling my panties beginning to dampen at the idea of parading myself around a lesbian bar dressed up in an sexy outfit.

After dinner, Hannah and I drove to Cheryl's Babeland store on Broadway, where she escorted us to a fitting room in the back of the store. After talking with Cheryl about what we had in mind, she disappeared into the back and brought out a few outfits for me to try on. The first few garments involved the predictable see-through lingerie sets and skimpy schoolgirl costumes, but when she brought us a full-length vinyl body suit with strategic hole placements, both of our eyes widened in excitement. Decorated with metal studs and large fabric cut-outs for the breasts, buttocks and crotch area, it left little to the imagination.

After I tried it on, Hannah's eyes opened as wide as saucers while she nodded at me with a huge grin on her face. Somehow, wearing this full-length shiny body suit made me feel even *more* naked by drawing attention to my private areas.

"Holy shit," she said, admiring me in the full-length dressing room mirror. "That is one shit-hot, smoking outfit."

"You can't possibly imagine me walking into a *public setting* wearing this thing?" I said, shaking my head as I turned my body around to examine just how revealing it was on both sides of my body.

"Um, actually," she smiled. "I can. Can you imagine the kind of interest you'll generate walking into a lesbian bar dressed up like that? Talk about a *chick magnet*. You'd have every butch-dyke hitting on you in no time."

"Not to mention most of the *other* girls in the bar," Cheryl nodded, coming into the dressing room to inspect my outfit. "But if you *really* want to attract the dommes and take your role-playing to the next level, I have one *other* accessory that'll finish this look off perfectly."

She disappeared back into the store, then returned with a studded leather collar and a long black leash.

"If you wore this with Hannah leading you on a tether, you'd leave zero doubt as to your position in the pecking order."

I paused for a moment, then looked at the two of them with an incredulous expression.

"Are you *kidding* me?" I said. "You think it'll be sexy leading me around like a dog on a *leash*?!"

"Well, you *did* say you wanted to see how far we could take this," Hannah smiled. "This would be pretty much taking it to the maximum degree."

"I've never really been in a lesbian bar before," I said. "What if everybody just wants to paw and molest me when they see me in this thing? Are you going to protect me if things get a little out of control?"

"Of course," Hannah said. "You're still my best friend. I wouldn't let anything happen to you that you didn't feel comfortable doing. But you shouldn't close your mind too much about exploring the possibilities with this scenario. You might actually *enjoy* the kind of attention you're likely to attract from certain members of the lesbian subculture.

"Just how dark does it *get* in these kinds of bars?" I said, peering at the bright overhead lights above me in the dressing room. "I'm going to feel pretty self-conscious if they can see my exposed body as easily as you can in here."

"It's a lot darker than *this*, believe me," Hannah said. "It *is* a pick-up bar, after all. There'll be a lot of extra-curricular activity going on in the corners. Don't worry–you won't be the *only* one attracting the attention of the circling wolves."

"Okay," I said, beginning to relax. "I'm willing to give it a try at least this once. I mean, how bad can it be, right? I'm the one who's ultimately in charge of what happens to my body."

"Exactly," Hannah said, turning her wrist to peer at her watch. "Come on. Let's get you home and lolled up to make you as irresistible as possible. I'm just as excited as you to witness the sexual dynamic in this situation.

After we drove back to Hannah's place, she had me sit down at her make-up table while she fussed over my mascara, eyebrows, and lipstick. After we were all done, we finished off the ensemble with a pair of six-inch-high stilettos, which I thought made me look even *more* like a cheap hooker.

"You're certainly not going to have any trouble attracting every red-blooded lesbian alpha in the room tonight," Hannah said, licking her lips at me. "I'd jump you *myself* right now if you weren't already bound up in that skin-tight costume."

I looked at Hannah with a raised eyebrow and smiled.

"There's still plenty of openings for you to have your way with me. Do you want to have another go with your big purple dildo?"

"Maybe later," Hannah chuckled. "Right now, I'm more excited to see how all the *other* lesbian women react to you. Let's go–it's getting close to prime time."

Hannah and I drove over to the East side where we pulled into a large parking lot next to an industrial building painted in all black. A small neon sign hung over the entrance door flashing *Sappho* in pink letters. I could see a small group of women dressed up in torn jeans and spiky colored hair loitering near the door smoking cigarettes. They looked at our car when we pulled up, then resumed talking amongst themselves.

"Are you sure this is a good idea?" I said, looking at the bare-armed, tattooed girls standing by the door.

"Of course," Hannah said. "It'll be fun. Just lose yourself in the role, and see how it plays out. If you're not digging it, let me know and we can take off whenever you've had enough."

"Okay," I said, wondering what the hell I'd gotten myself into.

Hannah fished around in her purse then pulled out the leather collar and attached it around my neck, snapping on the leather leash and opening her door.

"You sit tight while I come around the other side to get you. If we're going to do this, we might as well play the roles to the full extent for the maximum effect."

"Yes, Master," I said, smiling at her with an obedient expression.

Hannah walked around to the other side of the car, then opened my door and picked up the leash, pulling me gently out of the car. When she led me around the back of the car and the women by the door caught sight of my outfit with Hannah leading me by the leash, everybody stopped talking and stared at me dumbfounded. Hannah simply pretended like everything was normal and walked nonchalantly past the crowd, nodding to a doorman who waved us past the door into the dark and noisy club.

When we entered the main room, there was a female impersonator singing a song on stage with a group of women dancing in the corner. As we headed over to the bar, all the girls milling nearby turned to look at the two of us, running their eyes up and down my body and staring at my exposed skin, which flashed like beacons under the overhead strobe light next to my blacked-out costume in the dark and musky room.

When we finally got to the bar, I tried to position myself in such a way to show the minimum amount of skin, but no matter which way I turned, I was either showing my bare-assed buttocks or exposed breasts and crotch.

"Jesus, Hannah," I said, cozying up to her as close as possible, trying to gain a modicum of cover. "This is even worse than I imagined. My exposed skin looks like its coated with fluorescent *paint* in this place. And everybody is staring at me!"

"I know," she smiled, motioning for the bartender to bring us some drinks. "Isn't it great? Don't you feel sexy dressed up showing off your best assets? If you wanted to play the submissive, this is your chance to test it on the ultimate stage. Just relax and enjoy all the attention. We've got the whole night ahead of us."

When the bartender arrived, Hannah ordered two mai tais and when he placed them on the counter in front of us, I grabbed one of the glasses, taking healthy gulp of the liquid courage.

"Just be cool, girl," Hannah said, pulling gently on my leash while wrapping her hand around the other end resting on the bar. "I got you. I mean, I really *got* you. No one's going to do anything either one of us wants them to do to you as long as they see who owns you."

"Okay," I said, beginning to feel the tension in my body relax as I shifted my weight slightly back from the bar. After a few minutes, a burly girl with a barbell stud in her lower lip approached the two of us, resting a heavily tattooed arm on the bar counter next to me.

"What's up, girl?" she said, glancing down at my protruding tits, pinched even tighter by the constricting black vinyl fabric. "That's quite a hot costume you're wearing."

"Um—thanks," I said, shifting my weight defensively to my other leg closest to Hannah.

"So what's your story?" she said, placing her other hand on my exposed ass while caressing my bare buttocks. "Are you two looking for a little fun, or is this a closed-loop kind of relationship?"

"That depends on what kind of mood my girl is in," Hannah said, eyeing the woman suspiciously while she looked down at her molesting hand disapprovingly. "She's *my* girl, but I might be interested in sharing the spoils if the mood strikes. What do you say, Jade? Do you want to find a private corner and explore some of the boundaries?"

I shifted my weight closer to Hannah while rubbing my body against her, signaling my interest in remaining fully under her control for the time being.

"I'm pretty happy staying with you right now, Master," I said, rubbing my ass against her hip to demonstrate my subordination.

"You heard the girl, *bitch*," Hannah said, swiping the woman's hand away from my ass. "Take your hands off her. This one's *mine*. Go find somebody else to play with."

"Whatever," the girl said, backing away from the bar and uttering a few curse words as she disappeared into the crowd.

"Well, I guess that's *one* way to attract the dominant wolves in the pack," I sighed, turning to take another gulp of my drink.

"You're not feeling the sexual energy so far?" she said, peering around at the other people in the bar.

"Not with *that* one at least," I said. "She was coming on a little too strong. Plus, she wasn't really my type. I don't mind mixing it up with a strong-minded woman, maybe just someone a little hotter, you know?"

"Yeah," Hannah nodded. "I get your drift."

She ordered another round of drinks, then yanked me gently by my harness, leading me across the room to a padded lounge in the corner of the bar where a group of attractive women were chatting amongst themselves and cheering while they watched the performer on the stage. As we approached their table, Hannah motioned with her head to gain their attention momentarily.

"Have you got room for two more?" she said. "We could use a more comfortable spot to sit down, and you girls look like you're up for a little fun."

"Absolutely, one of the women with shorter hair said, pushing the rest of the girls over to make room for us in the middle of the circular seat cushion. "Feel free to get nice and cozy right here between the group of us. It's got the best view of the stage."

Hannah squeezed past the girls on one side of settee, pulling me by the leash as I followed her submissively, taking a spot framed by the first girl and another one with tattooed arms beside me.

"I haven't seen you two in here before," the lead girl sitting next to Hannah said. "Were you just looking to take in the show, or were you looking for a *different* kind of action?"

"We're just kind of playing it as it goes," Hannah said, glancing over at the performer on the stage vamping it up as she sang the Melissa Etheridge anthem Come to my Window. "She's pretty good. She kind of even *looks* a bit like Melissa Etheridge."

"That's the whole idea," the girl said, holding her hands over her crotch like she was grabbing a cock. "But everybody knows she's got some *different* equipment to work with."

"Yeah, I can see that," Hannah said, noticing the singer's Adam's Apple bobbing up and down while she sang.

"Not like your *friend* here," the girl said, staring at my exposed tits poking out above the table. "She's got *all* the right equipment to work with."

Hannah peered over at me silently to see if I was receptive to the obvious advances of the girl, and I smiled at her blankly, taking another swig of my drink. The two alcoholic beverages were already making me a bit tipsy having only eaten a small salad all day, and I slumped back in the chair, resting my head against the padded backrest. Taking this as a signal of receptivity, the girl sitting next to me raised her glass off the table, rubbing it gently against my exposed nipples. I enjoyed the sensation of the cool surface against my skin, and I slunk further down in my chair, feeling my nipples harden from the combined stimulation of the chilly glass and the rest of the girls watching me from the other side of the table.

"Mmm," the girl next to me hummed, glancing over at Hannah. "I think she likes this. I bet she's a very attentive slave when you need her to be."

"When I *want* her to be," Hannah said, winking at me playfully.

"Oh yeah?" the girl said, reaching her other hand under the table. "What does she like to do? Or should I say, what is she best at *giving*?"

"She's good at *everything*, when she's in the right mood," Hannah smiled. "Am I right, Jade? You kind of *like* it when someone else is in charge, don't you?"

I nodded demurely as I felt the girl's warm hand caressing my bald pussy, running her fingers gently up and down my moistening slit. As her fingers danced over my clit, I couldn't help spreading my legs further apart, getting increasingly turned on by all the attraction around the table. It was kind of fun being the center of attention in our corner of the room, and I could feel my pussy getting wetter and wetter as the rest of the girls' eyes widened while they licked their lips as my seatmate played with my pussy.

After a few minutes of teasing me with her fingers, she grew increasingly bold with her exploration, and when I began to rock my hips in appreciation of what she was doing, she suddenly thrust three fingers deep into my cunt and began ramming her hand hard against my crotch as she leaned over to suck on my nipples into her mouth. I could feel myself getting increasingly turned on by all the stimulation in the public setting, and as I began to moan softly and begin to gyrate in my seat, two of the girls on the other side of the booth ducked underneath the table and crawled toward me, licking and nibbling on the insides of my legs.

They pushed my knees further apart and when their mouths reached my now-dripping pussy, the girl next to me removed her fingers from my hole, allowing the other girls to lick and lap up my juices in a combined two-person assault on my snatch. When the girl beside me began to pinch one of my hardened nipples and flick her fingernail against the flexing teat, the girl sitting next to Hannah couldn't resist any longer and reached over in front of her, rolling my other nipple hard between her fingers. Without any sign of protest on my part, she crawled overtop of Hannah who saw that I was enjoying all the attention, then she straddled my hips facing toward me as she ground her hips into my hard mound.

At first, I enjoyed the combined attention of the swarming mob, but as they grew increasingly rough and bold with their exploration of my body, I began to tense up. While I enjoyed the stimulation from a sexual point of view, I was beginning to feel a bit claustrophobic in the tight confines of the cloistered booth, and I began to pull my thighs together to deter the two women under the table from taking any further liberties.

But instead of reading my signal to back off, they yanked my legs even wider apart while taking turns ramming their fingers into me and lapping up the juices coating the inside of my thighs. When the butchy girl on top of me began kissing down the side of my neck and biting the muscle on top of my shoulder hard enough to cause me pain, I started to push back, trying to signal that I was beginning to feel uncomfortable with how they were taking advantage of me.

But between the action of the girl on top of me pulling me hard against the back of the cushion with her outstretched arms and the girl next to me pinching my nipples tightly and the two girls under the table taking turns ramming their fingers into me up to their knuckles, I was began to panic, and I pushed back more forcefully against the woman pinning me to the cushion while trying to close my thighs against the combined strength of the two women under the table.

When Hannan saw the panic in my eyes and my desperate attempts to free myself from the combined press of the four women, she reached out to the girl sitting on top of me, temporarily pulling her shoulders away from my pinned body.

"I think my girl's had enough of your attention for the time being," she said. "Can't you read the signals? I think she wants you to back off."

"I haven't heard her say stop yet," the girl on top of me said, yanking her body back against my torso with her strong arms, pressing me tightly against the back of the cushion.

"What do you say, Jade?" Hannah said, looking at me to affirm her suspicions. "Have you had enough for now?"

"Yes," I said. "This getting to be a bit too much."

"You heard the girl," Hannah said, trying to pull the big girl's shoulders away from me.

"*Back off*, bitch," she said, swiping Hannah's hand away forcefully. "*You're* the one that brought this slave into our booth. You can have her back when we're finished with her."

"I'm sorry but that doesn't work for me," Hannah said, suddenly grabbing the woman's hair with two hands and yanking her backwards toward the table. "You heard the lady. No means no."

With her nostrils flaring and her eyes filled with rage, she slammed the girl's head hard against the top of the wooden table, momentarily stunning her. Then Hannah stood up on the settee, kicking the woman's head sitting next to me, snapping it backwards. Then she scampered over the top of the table and pulled the woman onto the floor in one swift move, glaring at the rest of the women around the table. Then she grabbed my hand and pulled me off the bench, freeing me from the grasp of the other two women under the table.

"Anyone *else* want to see who's in charge here?" she glared at the rest of the stunned girls sitting around the table. "Come on, baby, let's get the fuck out of this dive. These aren't the kind of chicks that deserve your attention."

Hannah unclipped the leash from my collar and threw it on the floor, then threaded her arm between mine and pushed her way through the club until we spilled out the exit door, breathing in the fresh air from the parking lot.

"I'm sorry, Jade," she said, peering at me as she pushed my ruffled hair to one side. "I didn't know things were going to get that quickly out of control in there."

"Yeah," I said, shaking my head, still in shock. "I think I've had my fill of this whole dom and submissive thing. Although I gotta say, you really turned me on with that whole alpha-wolf, kick-ass performance in there. Where did *that* come from?"

"I just kind of lost control when I saw how they were taking advantage of my best friend and starting to hurt you. I'd never stand by when I saw someone trying to do anything to you that you weren't enjoying."

"Thanks, hun," I said, throwing my arms around her. "Can we go home now and make love the way we used to? You know, when neither one of us is thinking about who's in charge or who's on the top or the bottom. I just want to make love like we're *equals* again."

"Absolutely," Hannah said. "I think I learned just as much from this little experiment as you. Ultimately, every successful relationship depends on mutual respect and consent. It's fine to play master and submissive every now and then, but only with the underpinnings of a real abiding love. Otherwise, it can quickly devolve into an unhealthy dynamic."

"I couldn't have said it better myself," I said, kissing her gently on the cheek. "Come on, there's someone *else* I feel like sharing the love with right now..."

VOLUME THREE

THE FIRST LADY

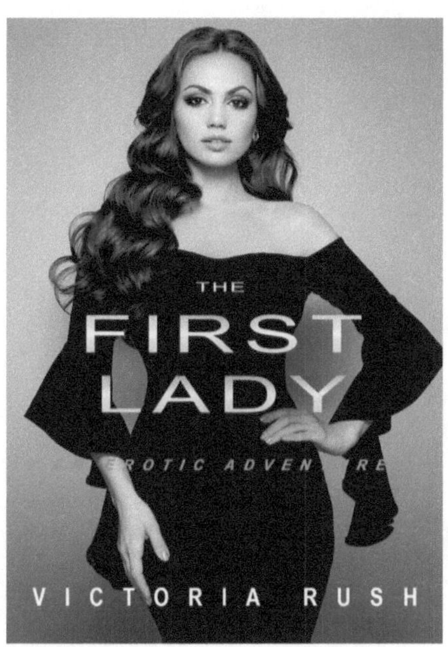

1

After a long day of schmoozing at my local political fundraiser, I dragged myself into the nearest Starbucks for a much needed break. I'd been invited to the event by the mayor's wife, and knowing that an election was just around the corner, I was eager to plant some seeds for potential work designing the team's campaign material. A commission helping to design their website and political banners would be a major feather in my cap and be a major stepping stone for networking with other bigwigs in the party apparatus. But after three straight hours of genuflecting and kissing ass, I needed some downtime to rest my brain and reclaim my soul.

After grabbing my almond-milk Americano at the pick-up counter, I ambled over to the one remaining seat in the corner of the shop, where an attractive woman sat alone nursing a warm beverage. It seemed odd to me that she was wearing a headscarf and sunglasses indoors, and although it was obvious that she wanted to be alone, I desperately needed to get off my feet.

"Do you mind if I take this last open chair?" I said, motioning to the chair directly opposite her.

"No, of course," she said distractedly, lost in thought.

"I'm sorry to intrude," I said, kicking off my shoes under the table. "But I've been standing all day and my feet are killing me."

"I know the feeling," the woman said, smiling half-heartedly.

Her face looked vaguely familiar, but it was hard to place her under her heavy camouflage. She looked to be about my age, maybe just a few years older, with wavy brown hair and perfectly coiffed, arching eyebrows. With her soft flushed cheeks and clear lip gloss coating her full sensuous lips, she could have easily passed for a matinee idol.

But it was her unusual *outfit* that attracted my attention the most. Wearing an off-the-shoulder, tight-fitting black chiffon dress with flared sleeves and sparkling diamond hoop earrings dangling from her ears, she definitely didn't look the part of the average Starbucks customer.

"You look like you could use a little respite from the elements too," I said. "What brings you into our community coffee shop on this cold wintry day?"

"Just needed a break from all the hubbub, I guess. A few too many boring meetings."

"*Meetings*?" I said, glancing down at her curvy figure outlined by her clingy dress. "If you don't mind my saying, you don't look dressed for a typical business meeting. I gotta say, you're *rocking* that dress."

"Thanks. They're not your typical business meetings. There's a lot of high-powered people. I guess I'm expected to look the part."

I caught her glancing in the direction of an adjacent table where two stiff young men dressed in gray business suits wearing earpieces watched her intently. I jerked suddenly when I began to put the pieces together. High powered business meetings. An important political convention in town. A classy woman dressed to the nines accompanied by a security detail. I had the crazy fortune to be sitting next to the President's wife!

"Oh my God!" I gasped. "You're the–"

"*Shh!*" she whispered, lowering her head and turning her body toward the corner of the room. "It's hard enough trying to maintain a low profile with these goons following me everywhere I go. Can we try to keep this little secret between the two of us?"

"Of course," I said, pushing back in my seat in shock. "I didn't mean to... It's just–"

"No worries," the First Lady said. "No need to get overly excited. I'm just another commoner in our humble little republic."

"I'd hardly call you that," I chuckled. "Even without all the trappings of political office, you're a long way from *common*."

"Thank you," she said, blushing slightly.

"Are you here for the Democratic fundraiser?" I asked. "I didn't see you at the convention center today."

"I try to leave all that political glad-handing to the big boys," she said. "I put in an appearance every now and then to demonstrate that all is happy and well with the first family and so the president can show off his eye candy, but otherwise I try to stay out of the affairs of the state as much as I can."

I peered at the First Lady through squinted eyes and nodded. It must have been tiring following her husband all around the country to various official functions, having to put on her game-face all the time. But there was something in her slack jaw and sad eyes that suggested there was a little more at work than just the harried life of a high-ranking political wife.

"I can appreciate that," I nodded. "Having spent enough time around all these politicos myself, I understand how exhausting it can be."

"What's *your* connection to the fundraiser, if I can ask?"

"I'm a freelance graphic designer. It's mostly a bunch of networking. There's a lot of money flung around these political campaigns. Just trying to get my small piece of the pie, I guess."

"These things tend to be pretty closed-door affairs," she said. "Do you mind my asking how you scored an invitation?"

"I know the mayor's wife in a roundabout way," I said, reflecting back on our little dalliance in the wine cellar of billionaire Steve Bannon's estate at last year's Halloween costume party.

"Haley's a doll," the First Lady nodded. "How do you know her exactly?"

"We're just casual friends," I fibbed. "I think she was just throwing me a bone as a favor, to be honest."

"Mm–hmm," she nodded, pinching her eyebrows together suspiciously. "What kind of design work do you do? Maybe I can throw you little bone, too."

"Oh, ah–" I stammered, momentarily taken aback by her generous offer. "Mostly website design, banners, logos, that sort of thing. It's kind of boring actually..."

"Are you kidding me?" the First Lady said. "Online fundraising has long since eclipsed the traditional form of fundraising by a large margin. I wouldn't sell yourself short. My husband needs to take advantage of every little edge he can find. Do you have any samples you can show me of your work?"

"Sure," I said, tapping my phone to pull up my photo portfolio and turning it around for the First Lady to see. "These are some of the corporate commissions I've worked on. There's no government applications to speak of, but some of my logo and signage work could be easily adapted for political purposes."

The First Lady took my phone out of my hand and began swiping her finger across the screen, nodding her head as she scrolled through my portfolio.

"These are actually pretty good," she said, pursing her lips in appreciation. "I think my husband's tired old campaign team could use some fresh ideas like these. Do you have a card I can pass along to our national campaign manager?"

"Wow, um–thank you," I stammered. "That's very generous of you."

"From the looks of some of these *other* pictures in your library, it appears that you know Haley a little more than just casually. Are these photos from Steve Bannon's infamous annual Halloween Ball?"

"Yes," I said, wrinkling my forehead at the thought of her viewing my personal pictures. "I got an invitation through a friend of a friend–"

Suddenly the First Lady's eyes flung open as she continued swiping through my photo library.

"Is this *you* wearing that provocative cowboy costume? You were really letting it all hang out at the costume party!"

I reached out and retrieved my phone, blushing a deep shade of crimson when I saw that she'd seen me dressed up in full regalia with my faux cock and balls dangling between my open leather chaps in the Lone Ranger costume.

"Bannon's invitation encouraged the guests to be creative and wear as little or as much as we desired. I guess I wanted to make a statement around all those self-absorbed high-rollers and show them that men aren't the *only* ones who can swing a big dick around."

"Humphh!" the First Lady coughed into her coffee, spilling some of it onto the table as she held out her hand to her security team to signal that she was okay.

"I like your style, young lady," she said, wiping up the table with a small serviette. "I think you're exactly the kind of free-thinking woman my husband needs on his starchy old campaign team. What's your name?"

"Jade," I said handing her my business card. "Jade Jackson. I'm not exactly sure how I should address you. Shall I address you as Madame First Lady?"

"*God*, no. Technically, I'm a private citizen, just like you. The job of First Lady refers a role, not a public office. So there's no need for such silly honorifics. You can call me Liz."

"It's a pleasure to meet you, Madame—I mean, Liz," I said, holding out my hand.

"The pleasure's all mine," Liz said, clasping my hand warmly.

We held onto each other's hand for a long moment, and I felt a buzz of electricity course through me while I watched her pupils dilating in excitement as another part of my body throbbed in arousal.

"How would you like to attend a different kind of fundraiser, at the White House next week?" she asked.

"Who–*me*?" I said incredulously. "You're inviting me to the *White House*?"

"Yes," she said. "The President's hosting his annual Correspondent's Dinner next Saturday and I could introduce you to a few people in his inner circle who might be interested in your services. Of course, you'll have to dress a little more conservatively than you did at Mr. Bannon's party. A ball gown might be more appropriate in this case."

"I think I could manage that," I said, clearing my throat. "But how do I get in? I'm sure there's exceptional security..."

"I'll send you an invitation with a special entry code. Just show your credentials at the guard shack. I'll leave your name for them to usher you in. Do you think you'll be able to make it?"

"I'm think I might be able to clear my schedule," I joked. "Thank you for your kind invitation."

"You can bring a partner with you if you'd like. I'll likely be pretty distracted with official duties at the affair, so I don't know how much attention I'll be able to give you. Just enjoy yourself and try not to ruffle any feathers. If you present yourself well enough, I'm sure we can connect you with the right people to further your career."

"Thank you. I look forward to seeing you again."

"That makes two of us," the First Lady said, motioning for her security team as she stood up to leave. "I'm looking forward to having you join the team. See you next Saturday."

As the First Lady gathered her belongings and swooped out the front door of the coffee shop with her security detail in tow, I sat back down on my chair with wobbly legs. I could scarcely believe what had just happened. Not only had I met one of the most intriguing and powerful women in America, she'd invited me into the White House to meet the President and his inner circle. But there was something *more* than that. I sensed we'd developed a powerful bond in the short time we'd been together, and I sensed she felt it too. I slumped back in my chair breathing a huge sigh, wondering what was in store with this sexy, beautiful woman.

2

On the day of the President's ball, I flew to Washington, D.C. then checked into a hotel to prepare myself for the big event. I didn't want to get all rumpled and sweaty flying in my dress clothes aboard a packed commercial airliner. Besides, it would look pretty strange boarding an aircraft in a ball gown and high heels.

The only gown I still had in my wardrobe was a frumpy old prom dress from twenty years ago, so I definitely felt the need to upgrade for such an important occasion. I wasn't sure how extravagant I should be, but Liz had told me to dress conservatively, so in the end I chose a midnight blue satin gown with a long pleated skirt and a V-neck bodice that revealed just enough of my cleavage to show off my best assets.

Gathered at the waist with a round bump in the rear, it was suitably understated and sexy at the same time. To finish off the look, I bought some black Christian Louboutin four-inch pumps with his trademark red lacquer sole. I didn't know if anyone would be looking down that far at the gala, but if they did, I didn't want them thinking I was so destitute that I'd blown an entire year's clothing budget on this one ensemble (which I very nearly had).

At two p.m., I went to my pre-arranged appointment at the city's premiere hair salon, where I sat for two hours with a stylist who created a flat wave design that looked minimal but still contemporary and chic. When I climbed out of the chair, my hair shone with a radiance that reminded me of my teenage years swimming in the lakes of Northern Wisconsin, where the clear waters and natural sunlight created a soft, natural look. I had just enough time after my appointment to get back to my hotel and put myself together for the scheduled start of the reception at seven o'clock.

When my taxi pulled up beside the White House, I walked up to the guard shack where a uniformed officer checked my credentials. After confirming my name on the guest list, he unlocked a heavy wrought-iron gate leading to a stone pathway adjacent to the curved central driveway. Signs pointed the way to the reception area, where randomly spaced Secret Service agents made sure I didn't stray off the marked path. When I reached the tall colonnaded Front Portico of the White House, I ascended the front steps barely believing I was entering the home of the President.

After stepping into the main entrance hall, ushers directed me down a long hallway lined with pictures of past presidents into a ballroom the size of an olympic swimming pool. Lined with floor-to-ceiling palladian windows and three enormous crystal chandeliers, the room sparkled in the glow of the late autumn sunset. But what really attracted my attention was the guest list. Milling about the packed ballroom I caught glimpses of Beyonce, George Clooney, Leonardo DiCaprio, Scarlett Johansson, and many other celebrities. Scattered among the clustered groups were various members of the President's inner cabinet, including the Secretary of State and the Vice President. But nowhere to be found was the First Lady.

Feeling isolated and exposed among the high-powered group of guests, I headed over to the bar where I ordered a stiff cocktail to calm my nerves. After a few minutes, a handsome local news anchorman sauntered over next to me to make small talk and begin flirting with me. As relieved as I was to have someone to talk to, there was really only one person I was eager to see. Gazing out at the milling movie stars and celebrities while the newsman continued pestering me with his lame pick-up lines, I wished I had the courage to join some of the other important people in the room.

After my third drink, I noticed a flash of red emerging from the middle of the crowd, and Liz caught my eye as she began walking in my direction. Wearing a clingy off-the-shoulder, crimson-colored gown with a long sweeping train, she showed off all the exquisite curves of her voluptuous figure. With her hair pulled back in a pretty French braid, she dominated the scene as the most beautiful woman in the room. Which was saying a lot, given the glittering guest list.

When she approached the bar, she smiled at me, motioning for the bartender to refresh her spritzer.

"Jade!" she said, flashing her pearly-white teeth as she clasped my hand warmly between hers. "I was afraid you didn't make it. I've been looking for you all evening."

"Are you *kidding*? I wouldn't miss this for anything. But I've been kind of hiding out here at the bar. I feel a little self-conscious mingling among all these famous people."

"There's no need to be shy," Liz said, glancing over at the hunky newsman still standing uncomfortably close to me. "Is this your date?"

"No," I grimaced. "I came alone. My preferences lean more in the feminine direction. But I felt self-conscious bringing a girlfriend with all the political implications and everything..."

"Nonsense!" Liz said, as my would-be paramour finally got the message and drifted off into the crowd. "Half the people in this room are gay or bisexual. Come on, let me introduce you to some interesting people."

She took my hand and led me to the other side of the room where I recognized some familiar political faces. She pulled me to the edge of one cluster and the group turned around to acknowledge her.

"Jade, this is Bill Holland, our national campaign manager. I've told him about some of the excellent work that you do and he was eager to meet you."

"Pleasure to meet you, Jade," Bill said, extending his hand. "The

First Lady mentioned you've worked on some high-profile corporate digital campaigns. We could use some fresh ideas to extend our reach into the ever-growing millennial group."

"I think Liz–I mean the First Lady–might be overselling my portfolio a tad, but I'd be happy to talk with you about some of the programs I've managed and how we might be able to adapt them to meet your needs–"

"*There* you are!" a deep voice suddenly interrupted us as a tall distinguished man in a black tux joined the group. I looked up to see the President smiling at Liz, and he stepped next to us, clasping her hand tightly. "I wondered where you'd scurried off to. I feel naked without my beautiful wife by my side."

He looked more handsome close-up than he appeared on TV, and with his broad shoulders and imposing size, he certainly looked the part of Commander-in-Chief.

"You didn't look so lonely chatting up Scarlett Johansson and Jennifer Lawrence on the other side of the room a bit earlier," Liz said with a wry smile.

"Just trying to keep our guests entertained, dear. It never hurts to be seen in the company of some of the key media influencers–am I right, Bill?"

"Being seen with high-profile celebrities definitely adds to your star power, Mr. President," Bill nodded, kowtowing to his boss.

"Speaking of," the President said to Liz. "There's someone I wanted you to meet. Warren Buffet's been one of our biggest campaign contributors, and he's been talking about making a big donation to one of your causes. He's just over there on the other side of the room–"

Liz jerked the President's hand as he began to pull her away.

"I'd like to introduce you to a friend of mine, first," she said, turning toward me. "Jade Jackson will be joining our campaign team and I really think she can help take your online fundraising efforts to the next level."

"Pleased to meet you, Jade," the President said, shaking my hand politely. "I'll look forward to talking with Bill about how you might be able to help us. But right now, I've got some other important matters to attend to." He peered at his wife with a steely expression. "Liz, will you join me?"

As I watched the President and the First Lady walk away from our group, I sensed a certain tension between the two of them, with Liz walking a half-step behind him with her arm outstretched as he pulled her along. She turned around and mouthed the words *see you later* to me, and I smiled and nodded passively toward her. I really didn't expect to see much of her again for the rest evening, except when the gala was over and the first couple bade farewell to their guests.

For the next five minutes or so, the campaign manager and I exchanged ideas on how to spruce up their online website, then he drifted away toward another group of heavy hitters. I was glad when the ushers announced that dinner was ready and began directing everyone into the adjacent State Dining Room. The room was filled with a collection of circular white-linen-covered tables festooned with gleaming crystal dinnerware and tall bouquets of fresh flowers. One of the ushers directed me toward a table half-way back from the Guest of Honor table with a small stage to the left, and he motioned for me to sit down in front of a tent card bearing my name.

I noticed the names of two other women in front of the adjacent chairs, and before long I was joined by the President's press secretary and the First Lady's chief of staff, straddling either side of me. They introduced themselves and made polite small talk while the rest of our table guests were seated, mostly comprising low-level press correspondents and administrative officials. The two women were both single and pretty, and I wondered if Liz had requested a last-minute seating adjustment after she'd heard I came without a date and that I had a sexual preference for women.

After the first course was served, the President stood to make a speech sprinkled with homilies praising the First Amendment while poking fun at some of his counterparts in the press. Then Jimmy Kimmel took the stage and launched into a monologue making good-natured jokes about the President and some of his more controversial political policies. It was all highly entertaining, and I enjoyed peering around the room at all the famous celebrities laughing and clapping along dutifully, but it was the First Lady who my attention was fixated on for most of the evening.

After Jimmy Kimmel finished his piece and the chairman of the correspondent's association took the stage to thank the attending newsmen and women for their journalistic integrity in a thinly veiled attempt to curry favor toward the incumbent President, I excused myself and asked to be pointed in the direction of the ladies' room. I didn't really need to use it, but all the political glad-handing was giving me an uneasy feeling in the pit of my stomach. I'd never been a strong proponent of any one political party, and all this genuflecting was making me rethink the whole idea of helping to push the President's agenda. Especially one who didn't seem to give his wife the proper respect and attention I felt she deserved.

After checking my makeup in the powder room mirror, I went into one of the cubicles and pulled out my phone, tapping on my favorite game of Candy Crush. I couldn't believe that I was attending the most coveted event in the most famous residence in Washington, and here I was sitting in a dingy cubicle playing a solitary video game. After a few minutes, I heard the clack-clack-clack of a woman's shoes entering the marble-floored restroom, and I peered under the door recognizing Liz's long red dress train.

I turned off my phone and held my breath while I listened to her attending to herself in the mirror, but it seemed to take an eternity for her to finish whatever she was doing. Feeling a bit self-conscious waiting for her to leave, I decided to flush the toilet and emerge from my hiding place to say hello. I didn't know when I'd have a chance to be this close to her again, and when she saw me emerge from the cubicle, she gave me a broad smile.

"Jade," she said. "I saw you head toward the washroom and when you didn't return, I grew worried about you. Are you enjoying the evening?"

"Yes," I lied. "It's fascinating watching all these beautiful people mingling, but to be honest I don't have much of a stomach for all this political maneuvering. I just needed to come in here and freshen up."

"I know exactly how you feel," Liz said. "Seeing all these rich and powerful people gushing over one another and self-congratulating themselves can get a bit tiring. You should try doing it twenty-four/seven, three hundred and sixty-five days a year."

"I can only imagine how difficult your job must be," I frowned. "You must feel like a prisoner sometimes locked up in this big fortress, having to play second fiddle to the most powerful man in the world."

Liz coughed, momentarily taken aback by my outspoken opinion.

"You seem to have a special insight on my unique predicament, Jade. Most people think I have one of the most glamorous jobs in America."

"I've been watching you most of the evening," I said. "It's not hard to see the signs of tension between you and the President."

"Is it *that* obvious?" Liz chuckled. "Have you at least been enjoying the company at your table? I hope Julie and Emma have been keeping you properly entertained."

"Yes, they've been lovely. But honestly, it's *you* that I haven't been able to take my eyes off the whole evening. You look absolutely ravishing in that form-fitting dress."

"As do you," Liz said, taking a step closer to me. "That blue satin gown complements your eyes perfectly. You look sexy and elegant at the same time. You chose well. Bill has already complimented me on how smart and creative you are. I hope you won't let all of this polit-ical backslapping get in the way of your helping with the campaign."

"I'll be happy to do it as a favor for you," I said, feeling my pussy flutter the closer she got to me. "Anything to keep me working close to you–"

Suddenly, Liz stepped forward and planted her lips against mine, running her fingers through my hair as she plunged her tongue deep into my mouth. I gasped at the unexpected intrusion, but as we pressed our bodies together and ground our pelvises against one another, I flung my arms around her, running my hands down over the curvature of her ass. She pulled me toward one of the cubicles while we continued kissing, then she locked the door behind us and slammed me against the metal partition wall.

While we groped each other's bodies pulling on each other's dresses, I pushed her back against the other side and slowly pulled up the hem of her long red gown. When I finally managed to hike it up over her hips, I snaked my hand between her legs and felt her panties soaked as wet as a dishrag. Pulling them to the side, I thrust two fingers deep into her slit and she threw her head back against the wall, grunting in pleasure.

"Oh Jade," she sighed. "You have no idea how much I've been dreaming of this from the moment I saw you. I haven't felt like this in such a long time..."

"You mean *wet*, or the touch of another woman?" I smiled, thrusting the palm of my hand firmly against her snatch.

"Wet, and *turned on*. James is such a passionless lover. The constant demands of his office have left me cold and dry for the longest time. You're the first woman I've been with this way."

"I'm glad we found each other," I said. "Because I haven't felt this turned on in a long time either."

"But you said you've been with other women–"

"Yes, but I haven't felt this strong a connection with anyone in a long, long time."

"Is it just because–"

"Like you said," I interrupted. "Being First Lady is a *role*, not a job. I like you for a million other reasons."

"We better do this quick then," she said, looking through the crack in the door. "Before my security detail begins to worry about me and checks up on me."

"Even in the White House washroom?!" I said.

"You have no idea how short a leash I have around here."

"Just lie back and enjoy it then," I smiled. "I want to make you feel pleasure you haven't experienced in a long time."

I knelt down slowly until I reached her midsection, then I placed the bottom half of her dress over my head while I pulled her panties down to her ankles. Then I leaned forward, engulfing her inflamed clit in my mouth, running circles over the hard nub while I curled my fingers inside her pussy toward her sensitive G-spot. It didn't take long for Liz to begin moaning more loudly, and as her pleasure began to inexorably rise, she placed her hands over the back of my head, caressing me softly while my tongue danced over her burning gland.

After about sixty seconds of sustained stimulation on her bulb, she lifted her right leg and tilted her pelvis toward my chin, pressing her pussy harder into my face. I could feel the inside of her vagina beginning to tent and I knew she was nearing the precipice, so I sucked her button hard into my mouth while fluttering my fingers against her G-spot. Within seconds, she gasped as her whole body lurched forward in a series of spastic jerks as the walls of her pussy pulsed firmly against my embedded fingers.

I held her gently in my mouth until her contractions stopped and her breathing began to return to normal, then I lifted myself up and kissed her gently on her lips. We heard the sound of another woman's shoes entering the room, and Liz lifted her finger to her lips signaling for me to be quiet while she peered through the crack in the door. Then she quickly pulled her panties back up and leaned in to whisper in my ear.

"It's one of my security guards," she said. "You'll have to wait in here while I pretend like I'm finishing up my business."

"Can I see you again?" I said, looking desperately into her eyes. I didn't want this little tryst to be the last time I saw her.

"I'll call you. Right now, I've got to get back to the function or the President will begin to worry and send his whole squad after me. Thank you Jade–you were even more magnificent than I imagined. Bye for now."

She gave me a little peck on the cheek, then opened the door partway and headed toward the sink to wash up. I peered through the crack and saw a pokerfaced woman with short cropped hair and a business suit nod toward her while she stepped back as Liz fixed her hair and makeup in the mirror. Then the two women exited the room as quickly as they had entered, leaving me alone and breathing heavily in my little cubicle. After they left, I tore off my panties and fingered myself to the quickest orgasm I'd had in ages while reliving the electric moment when I felt the First Lady's warm, pulsing flesh in my hands.

I didn't know when I'd see her again, but at this precise moment I felt like I'd lived a thousand years in the blink of an eye.

3

After the dinner finished and the guests began streaming out of the White House, I joined the long line where the President and First Lady thanked everyone for coming and bade them farewell. When it was my turn to face them, the President shook my hand politely and Liz winked at me, saying she was looking forward to working with me on her husband's campaign. When I got back to my hotel, I must have come a hundred times replaying the erotic scene from the White House powder room over and over again.

But the following morning, I woke up uneasily, wondering if the whole thing was just some bizarre fantasy. The President hadn't even remembered talking to me earlier in the evening, and his campaign manager had made no attempt to reconnect with me before leaving the building. Having not heard back from Liz and not knowing when or if she'd contact me again, I began to pack up my belongings to leave the hotel before check-out time. But just as I was about to close the door behind me, I heard the phone ring and I scurried back inside to pick it up.

"Hello?" I said breathlessly, pouncing on the bed.

"Jade?" a familiar voice said. "It's Liz. I wanted to call you before you left town. Did you enjoy the party last night?"

"Yes, of course," I said. "But it was all a bit of a blur, really. I felt a little out of my element around all those celebrities and high-powered political figures. Except when I was with *you* of course. I haven't been able to get you out of my mind ever since our little rendezvous in the restroom."

"Me too," Liz said. "I can't bear the idea of you returning home so soon. I was wondering if you'd like to meet up for lunch so we can continue our discussion about your helping with the campaign team."

"At the White House?" I said, wondering if she was going to invite me back into her inner sanctum.

"It would be better to meet you alone, where we won't be disturbed by the President's minders. Can I meet you at your hotel?"

"Of course," I said, feeling my pussy beginning to flutter at the thought of being alone with her again. "I'm staying at the Marriott Marquis, downtown. Would you like to meet in the lobby?"

"I'd rather see you privately, away from all the prying eyes of the press and the public. What room number are you staying in?"

"1402," I said, feeling my panties beginning to moisten, hoping we'd have a chance to pick up where we left off.

"Will two p.m. work for you?"

"I'd wait until the end of time to see you again," I said, elated to hear that she wanted to meet me again.

"I was hoping you'd say that," Liz said. "See you soon!"

After she hung up, I called downstairs to extend my check-out time, then I went back into the washroom to touch up my makeup. I wasn't sure if Liz had the same thing in mind that I did, but I wanted to make myself as irresistible as possible to maximize my chances.

The next three hours passed by agonizingly slow as I tried to pass the time catching up on my email and browsing through stories of the First Lady's public appearances and personal causes. When I read that her personal passion and primary cause was helping spread the word about the importance of animal rescues, I felt even closer to her. Not only was she drop-dead gorgeous with a body to die for, she also had a heart of gold.

Shortly after the appointed hour, I heard a soft tap on my hotel room door, and I peered out the peephole to see Liz looking back at me, glancing from side to side nervously. I opened the door and invited her in, then closed the door softly behind us. She melted into my arms immediately, and we pressed our bodies together, kissing passionately.

"You're going to smear all your lipstick," I said, pulling away momentarily. "What about lunch–"

"*Screw* lunch," she said. "I'm feeling hungry for something *else* right now. Besides, we won't have much time before my husband begins to wonder where I've gone..."

"Doesn't he have more important things to worry about?" I said, shaking my head.

"You'd think so," Liz frowned. "But he's always been overprotective of me and a bit jealous of other people stealing my attention. I suspect it has something to do with his incessant need to be in control."

"What about your Secret Service detail? Won't they suspect what we're up to if we stay in here too long?"

"They've learned to mind their own business and respect my boundaries. Besides, my lead agent probably already knows we've got something going on after she walked in on us in the White House washroom last night."

"We better get *busy* then," I smiled, pulling Liz closer to my king-size bed.

"You have no idea all the ways I've been dreaming of making love to you since you left last night."

"Oh, I think I might have an idea or two," I said, pulling the bedspread down and throwing her onto the mattress. "I've been replaying this moment in my mind pretty steadily for at least the last twelve hours."

While the two of us groped and kissed each other awkwardly, we pulled on each other's clothes and undergarments until we were both naked on the cool hotel room sheets.

"Oh my God," I gasped, seeing her fully exposed for the first time. "You're even more beautiful than I imagined underneath that sexy ball gown. I've been undressing you with my eyes from the moment I saw you. I had no idea you'd be as exquisite as this."

Liz was tall and slender, with the tight, toned figure of a ballerina, her long legs seeming to go on forever. Her hips curved sexily around her bare mound, tapering to a narrow waistline, before flaring again to reveal perfectly shaped, full breasts that glistened in the bright morning light streaming through the sheer curtains of my hotel room. Devouring her like she was the last person on earth, I took her erect teats into my mouth and sucked on them voraciously while squeezing her firm tits between my hands.

"Jade," she panted, arching her back to lift her bosom toward my mouth. "God, how I've dreamed about feeling your lips on my skin again."

"My *fingers* weren't cutting it last night?" I teased, nibbling on her hard nipples with my teeth.

"Oh, they were *cutting* it, alright," she purred. "I liked the way you parted my folds and made me squeal like a little girl."

"You don't look so much like a little girl right *now*," I said, nibbling my way down her stomach while I caressed her firm mounds with my hands.

"*Hey*," she said, grabbing the sides of my head and pulling me back up toward her face. "It's my turn to return the favor. If *anyone's* going down on anybody in the little time we have together, it's gonna be me."

"Just how much time have we got?" I said, peering into her eyes with a wrinkled brow.

I'd hoped that her meeting me in the privacy of my hotel room would give us more time to explore each other than in the hurried and confined space of the White House restroom.

"I dunno, maybe a couple of hours—"

"That's plenty enough time for us to pleasure one another any *number* of ways. Why don't we try stimulating ourselves *together* before we start worrying about who's looking after whom?"

"I like the sound of that," Liz said, wrapping her legs around my ass while I moved up higher on her body, grinding my pelvis into hers as we kissed each other passionately.

With her hips tilted slightly upward, my bald pubis rubbed against her flaring clit, and she moaned into my mouth. I could feel her wet juices coating my mound as I ground my hard symphysis into her sopping slit while my own juices began pouring down the insides of her thighs.

"Oh God, Jade," Liz moaned. "You feel so good between my legs. Fuck me with that beautiful pussy of yours."

Up to this point, I would have been perfectly happy to bring her to orgasm without paying much attention to my own needs. But when she started talking dirty to me, I reached down and pulled her legs upward, pushing them far to the sides while I lifted myself up and squatted over her, mashing my dripping pussy onto her slippery slit.

"Holy shit!" Liz gasped. "*Fuck*, yes! Fuck my pussy with your hot cunny. You feel amazing–"

I leaned forward, kissing her passionately while we pressed our tits together, dancing our tongues in each other's mouths. While we rolled our hips against one another rubbing our nubs together, I arched my back and pressed my sex harder against her. I could hear the sound of our two voices moaning with increasing urgency as the sound of our wet pussies slapping together filled the room, and I wondered if her Secret Service agent was standing outside the door once again listening to all the noise we were making. But at this moment, that was the last thing I wanted to focus on as I reveled in the sights and sounds of this beautiful woman writhing and moaning underneath me.

As we rolled our slick lips together, I could feel Liz press her hips harder against mine while her grunting and breathing escalated in pitch and velocity. Suddenly, she dug her fingernails hard into my back and jerked her body in a series of spastic heaves as she moaned into my mouth.

"Yes, Jade!" she groaned. "I'm cumming, baby! Oh God–I'm cumming so hard in your hot, sweet pussy. Come with me!"

When she told me she was falling over the precipice, all the tension that had been building up inside me suddenly released like the floodgates of a dam, and I began gushing all over her flapping pussy as one powerful contraction after another began consuming me. I held her close while we pulsed against one another, fucking each other's mouths with our tongues.

It seemed to take forever for us to stop cumming together, but when the waves of pleasure finally subsided, I collapsed beside Liz and kissed her gently on her neck, breathing on her pinched nipples standing pertly atop her mounds like two alert sentries.

"Holy shit!" Liz panted. "I've never been made love to like that in my entire life."

"Because you've never been made love to by another *woman* before?" I said.

"No–because I've never been with anybody who exhibited that kind of passion before. It's like comparing a filet mignon with third-grade hamburger."

"I'm not sure the President would like to hear you referring to him as third-rate hamburger."

"Well, when it comes to lovemaking, I hate to say it, but that's kind of how I feel. Though he may have a number of other admirable qualities, he's never been terribly attentive or giving in the bedroom."

"Maybe he just feels the weight of the world on his shoulders..."

"Maybe," Liz said. "But I think it's a lot more than that. We just never seemed to develop that spark. I think he always viewed our union as more of a political expediency than a match made in heaven."

"So where does that leave us now?" I said, wondering how we'd ever be able to reconcile our rapidly growing attraction to one another with her continuing role as First Lady.

"Well, I don't know about you, but I'm in no hurry to end this. I can't imagine our going our separate ways, regardless of whatever working arrangement you set up with our campaign manager."

I peered at Liz with a pained expression, hoping to separate our professional relationship from our personal one.

"Isn't there some way we could find a way to work more closely together? At least close enough that we can find some more private time to be together like this?"

Liz paused for a moment while she considered the possibilities.

"There might be *one* way," she said as a sly smile formed on the outside corners of her lips. "Normally, the campaign team works out of their own headquarters on the other side of town. But I might be able to find a space for you to work in the East Wing if you'll be doing mostly solo design work on the website. I've already told the President we're friends. I think I can persuade him to carve out a space for you on my side of the executive wing if I beg and plead hard enough."

As excited as I was to hear her proposing to find me a permanent position at the White House, I couldn't help worrying about the implications of our involvement with her continuing relationship with her husband.

"I don't want you to overstep your bounds," I said. "I wouldn't want the President to suspect we've got something more serious going on than just a working relationship..."

"He's far too wrapped up trying to save the world and being the President of Everything to notice. Once I've got you installed in the White House, we'll have plenty more opportunities to carry on our little affair."

"Okay," I said, looking at her like a child who'd just had an ice cream cone pulled away from her. "But is that all you see this as–an *affair*?"

"Of course not. I didn't mean it that way. Right now, I can't imagine being separated from you for more than a millisecond. I haven't felt this way with someone in the longest time–perhaps *ever*. I see your job, as much as I honestly think you can help my husband's campaign, as really just a cover to keep us together. Let's take this one day at a time and see how it plays out. Once my husband is out of public office, we'll have more opportunities to explore taking our relationship to the next level."

I shook my head, realizing the irony of my helping to get him re-elected, knowing full well it would just make the hiding of our relationship all the more difficult.

"Okay, but I wouldn't want to drive a wedge between the two of you–"

"Don't worry about any of that right now," she mewed. "Let's just enjoy what we've created and savor the time we have together. Life's too short to worry about the pitfalls of following your heart."

Liz suddenly rolled on top of me, spreading my legs apart as she pressed her moist pussy against mine once again.

"But speaking of *wedges*," she grinned. "I wouldn't mind getting another piece of this before we have to separate for a little while..."

4
____

The following morning, Liz invited me back to the White House, where she greeted me at the front portico then walked me down a long corridor, pointing out some of the areas of interest.

"To your right is the Kennedy Garden, which is a lovely place for an outdoor lunch when the weather is good."

I gazed out the tall windows lining the colonnade at the immaculately manicured garden with its pretty holly trees and colorful flower beds.

"And to the left," she said, opening a door to a large room with a giant screen and plush theater chairs, "is the Family Theater Room."

"Did you and the President ever consider having children?" I asked, peering into the cavernous space.

"We just never got around to it, I guess. With his busy schedule, we feared there wouldn't be enough time to give the kids, and he seemed far more interested in his political career than building a family.

"That's too bad," I said, peering down the long hallway with all its nooks and crannies. "This looks like the ultimate playground for young children, and with all the support staff at the White House, you'd have lots of help caring for your children."

"I suppose," Liz said. "But with the current strain on our marriage, I'm not so sure about our prospects for staying together. I'd never want to subject them to a messy public divorce..."

I looked at Liz with sad eyes, realizing how much she felt like a prisoner in her own home. With all the eyes of the world focused on her and her husband, it must have been extraordinarily difficult for her to keep up appearances when she felt so unhappy.

When we reached the end of the corridor, we entered another large building and turned right down another long hallway.

"This is the East Wing," she said. "Which officially houses my office."

"This looks like a pretty big building for *one* person's office," I said, peering up at the tall ceilings and imposing pictures on the wall.

"It also houses a few other functions like the office of the White House social secretary, the Calligraphy Office, and the correspondence staff. But fortunately for you, unlike the West Wing where the President and his staff work, there's a lot of unused space in this building."

Liz stopped near the end of the hall and turned to open an oak door leading into a large, brightly lit office.

"This is my office, with a nice view of the garden and the South Lawn. I keep the door open most of the time, and you're welcome to come visit me anytime you have any questions or you just want some company."

I looked at Liz with a raised eyebrow and smiled.

"Knowing the kind of trouble we seem to get into when we're together, you might want to rethink that open-door policy..."

"You might be right about that," she said. "Fortunately, I'm about as far from the President during working hours as one can possibly be on this big estate, and he rarely comes down this way. So if you're feeling lonely any time, don't hesitate to barge in."

I peered around her office at the pretty paintings and the various artifacts arranged on her shelves. Prominently displayed on her desk and shelves were various photos of her and the President at various stages in his career. I picked up a wedding picture of the two of them on an adjacent shelf and smiled.

"You both look so handsome in this picture," I said.

"And *happy*," she said. "Those were our carefree days, before James started his political career."

"How old were you when you married?"

"Not long after college," she said, taking the picture from my hand and peering at it with sad eyes. "We met at Yale, where he was studying law at the time. I thought he was so dashing and handsome back then."

"He still *is*," I said, beginning to wonder if it was such a good idea for me to be working so close to her when she obviously still had feelings for her husband. "Where were you thinking of putting me up?"

"Oh," she said, putting the picture back on the shelf softly. "I almost forgot. I moved a few things around and put you in the office two rooms down. Come, let me show you."

Liz led me across the hall to a room on the other side of the building and opened the door, inviting me to step in. It was modest in size, but a large window streamed in bright sunshine, and the tall bookcases lining the walls made it look much larger than it was.

"It's not quite as big as my office," she said. "But you've got a nice view facing south and all the equipment you need to get you started on your project. I've left the login information for the computer on your desk. Bill has already sent you an email with some suggestions for updating the website. I've left his number in your Rolodex, so you can reach out with any questions at any time. Is there anything I can do for you before you get started?"

I looked around me at all the official trappings, feeling my heart beating a hundred miles an hour, suddenly feeling conflicted about my new role.

"Liz," I said, turning toward her with a furrowed expression. "I'm not so sure this is a good idea–"

"Shh," she said, placing her finger on my lips. "I'm sure this all seems overwhelming at this point. You'll have the support of my personal staff whenever you need anything–"

"No, it's not that," I said. "I could do this work just as easily from home, or from the campaign office for that matter. Are you sure–"

"Don't get cold feet on me now," Liz said, stepping forward to hug me gently. "I don't want you thinking you're getting in the way of James's and my marriage. It's been a marriage of convenience for a long time now. For all I know, he's carrying on an affair behind *my* back too. I want you here next to me. Give it a few weeks at least. If you don't feel as strongly about us being together as I do, I'll understand and we'll go our separate ways. But don't give up on this yet."

"Okay," I sighed. "I suppose it can't hurt to work on the campaign website for a little while, at least until we've revamped it according to the President's liking..."

"That's my girl," Liz said, raising my chin and kissing me sweetly on the lips. "Take your time easing into this. There's a kitchen at the other end of the hall where you can help yourself to coffee and snacks. Let's plan on having dinner together when you finish up today. I have some special plans for us later this evening."

After Liz returned to her office, I sat down at my computer and logged in, reading the long email from Bill Holland providing instructions on how he wanted the campaign website tweaked. Most of the suggestions made sense, and I tried to keep busy developing new design ideas for the next couple of hours. But I found myself becoming increasing distracted as the day went on, peering out the window at the large White House lawn with all the groundskeepers and Secret Service agents milling about. The more I thought about it, the more convinced I became that I'd gotten myself into a situation that could only end with someone hurt.

How could Liz and I hope to carry on our clandestine affair with all these staff and security people constantly milling about? Was our relationship destined to be another flash-in-the-pan, ignited by the undeniable passion we both felt for one another, but doomed to extinguish under the constant pressure and demands of her role as First Lady? What if our relationship *did* grow to become something deeper and more meaningful? How could she ever hope to extricate herself from the expectations of a watchful nation? America was just starting to acknowledge the idea of gay couples, but accepting a lesbian *ex-First Lady* was a whole other matter.

By the end of the day, I was having serious second thoughts about my continuing role in her life and thinking of heading home. But when Liz poked her head into my office around 4:30, she didn't give me a chance to tell her what I was thinking.

"Are you hungry?" she said. "The White House chef makes a mean stroganoff."

"I don't know Liz," I frowned, not quite ready to tell her I was thinking about leaving. "Maybe it's best I head back to the hotel..."

"At three hundred dollars a night? You'll go broke if you try living out of a hotel in this town. I insist. You simply *must* have a sit-down dinner at the White House at least once. Besides, there was so much more I wanted to show you–"

"Will the President be joining us?"

"He's got a late cabinet meeting that will keep him busy for another couple of hours. It'll just be the two of us. Come," she said, pulling me out of my chair. "Let me show you some more interesting parts of the White House."

For the next hour or so, Liz gave me a grand tour of the three floors of the grand residence, pointing out special points of interest such as the library and bowling alley on the ground floor, the beautifully appointed Red, Green, and Blue rooms on the State Floor, and the personal bedrooms and family dining room on the third floor. After showing me the master bedroom and personal living quarters on the top floor, she led me into the Yellow Oval Room, which led out onto the curved balcony of the South Portico overlooking the enormous South Lawn with its sparkling fountain and the Washington Monument rising majestically in the distance. The sun was setting to the west, and the white obelisk glistened with an orange hue in the fading dusk.

"It's magnificent," I said, looking at the picturesque setting with my mouth agape. "How could you ever grow tired of this view?"

"Well, you know what they say. Home is where the heart is. I'm afraid there hasn't been much warmth in this home these past three years. But enough of the depressing news. Come–let me show you where you'll be staying tonight..."

"*What?*" I said, peering at Liz with a shocked expression. "You want me to spend the *night* here?"

"By the time we finish dinner, it'll be too late for you to find another place to stay. Besides, who hasn't wanted to spend a night in the famous Lincoln Bedroom?"

5

—————

Liz grabbed my hand and led me back inside, where we turned into a large sitting room on the other side of the Yellow Room leading into a huge boudoir dominated by a large four-poster bed and a stone fireplace. Gold velvet curtains framed the two large picture windows, with tasteful Victorian-era chairs and settees placed around the foot of the bed.

"*This* is the Lincoln Bedroom?" I said with wide eyes. "It's even bigger than the *President's* bedroom!"

"Well, technically, they're the same size. Ours just has a bit more closet space. But yeah, it's pretty big, especially for one person."

Liz stepped toward me and kissed me hard on the mouth, thrusting her tongue inside my cavity.

"But we might be able to solve that problem with a little extra company."

Suddenly, I felt dizzy from the bombardment of my senses, and I went limp while she held me. As much as I'd wanted to run away from her only a short while ago, I was suddenly at her mercy, with all the same feelings and cravings circulating inside me.

"Liz," I tried to protest. "This is seriously too much. I don't deserve any of this."

"Nonsense," she said. "You've rekindled a passion and a joy for living that I haven't felt in ages. It's the *least* I can do to repay the favor. Besides, having you stay overnight gives us the perfect excuse to steal away when the mood strikes..."

She pushed me toward the bed and lay me down on the soft mattress, pushing my thighs apart with her knee as she looked at me with a devilish grin.

Suddenly, a loud ding sounded, and Liz turned around, frowning.

"That's the dinner bell. We better not keep our chef waiting. The staff's gone to a lot of trouble to prepare us a special meal, and we'll want to catch it while it's still hot. There'll be plenty of time for more play time later. Come–I'm famished!"

Liz led me to the northwest corner of the top floor to the family dining room, where the kitchen staff had prepared three place settings. The two of us sat down kitty-corner at the end of the table, where the staff proceeded to serve us a delicious three-course meal. By the time we'd finished, the sun had begun to set and I glanced out over the front lawn of the White House with its pretty, illuminated fountain. Just then, the President entered the room and peered at me with a surprised expression.

"I didn't know we were expecting *company* this evening," he said, obviously irritated.

"It's Jade's first day working on the campaign, dear," Liz said. "I set up a special office for her in the East Wing, and we were working a bit late. I thought I'd show her around and invite her to enjoy Pierre's specialty of the house. Since you were tied up in meetings and all..."

"Of course," the President said, pulling up a seat on the opposite side of the table next to Liz. "Is there anything left over for me? I didn't realize how hungry I was until I smelled the beef stroganoff."

"No trouble, Mr. President," the chef said, bringing another serving into the room and placing it in front of him with gloved hands. "And of course, we've saved an extra serving of your favorite dessert, crème brûlée."

"Thank you, Pierre," the President said. "You always know the best way to a man's heart."

"My pleasure, Mr. President," the chef said, backing into the adjacent kitchen.

"So how did you find your first day working in the White House?" the President said, peering at me as he took a mouthful of creamy pasta.

"It was all a bit overwhelming," I said, still hardly believing I was sitting down to have dinner with the President and the First Lady in their private dining room. "Liz has been such a gracious host and has provided me with *more* than I need."

The President looked at me suspiciously, then glanced over at Liz and smiled.

"How long have you known each other?" he said. "Liz said you were friends."

"Not that long actually," I blushed. "We met when you were attending the political convention in Chicago last week."

"You two seem to have formed an unusually strong bond in such a short period of time," he said. "Normally, Liz takes quite a while to warm up to new acquaintances. You must have made an especially powerful first impression."

"When Jade told me about the digital design work she's done," Liz interjected, "I thought it would be a perfect fit for our campaign. We just struck up a conversation and one thing led to another. We have a lot of the same interests and passions—animal rescue, AIDS research, gender equality..."

"It's good to have *passions*," the President said, nodding toward Liz. "I haven't seen the First Lady this animated about anything in a long time. Will you be staying with us long?"

"Actually, I've invited Jade to spend the *night*," Liz said. "She's a long way from home and I thought it would be fun for her to experience staying in the Lincoln Bedroom for one night. You know, something to tell her kids about someday..."

The President peered down at my right hand and cocked his head.

"Oh? Do you have children, Jade? I don't see a wedding ring."

"No, my first husband and I never got around to it. We split up long before the idea crossed our mind."

"So you're *single* then?" he said. "We've got lots of eligible young bachelors working in various administrative capacities in the West Wing. Perhaps you'd like to work on the *other* side of the executive campus where all the action happens–"

"I think Jade is perfectly happy with her *present* arrangements, dear," Liz interrupted. "It's getting late. I think I'll show Jade to her room and get her set up. Will you be coming up to bed soon?"

"I've got a late meeting with my chief of staff," the President said. "I'll join you in another hour or so."

Then he looked at me with a penetrating gaze.

"I hope you have a pleasant sleep, Jade. I'm looking forward to seeing some of your new work in the days ahead."

"Thank you, Mr. President," I smiled. "It will be my pleasure. I hope you like some of the new designs I've been working on."

"I'm sure I *will*," he said, stealing a quick glance down the top of my partially unbuttoned blouse.

After the President left to return to his office, Liz and I went back across the hall to prepare my room.

"That was kind of *scary*," I said to Liz when she closed the door behind us. "Do you think he has any suspicions what we've been up to?

"I think he's far too focused on his own self-important work to dream about any mischief going on behind his back."

Liz suddenly stepped forward, pushing me back down onto the mattress, then she climbed on top of me, spread-eagling her legs around my stomach. "But now that you mention it, there was one other dessert course I was looking forward to having before we turn in."

"Right *here and now*? In the *Lincoln Bedroom*?!"

"You wouldn't be the first guest to enjoy a little late-night tryst while sleeping over at the White House. It's kind of like being a member of the mile-high club. It's on every social climber's bucket list in this city."

"But I'm not a social climb–"

"I know," Liz said, beginning to unbutton my blouse. "That's just another thing I love about you. You don't have a selfish bone in your body. And you're not the least bit political. It's refreshing to have someone like you hanging around this ivory tower."

"Are you sure we've got enough *time*?" I said, peering nervously toward the closed door.

"He said he'd be gone at least an hour," Liz smiled. "That gives us plenty of time to enjoy a turn or two. Besides, there's something I've been dreaming about doing to you..."

Liz unbuttoned the rest of my blouse and removed my bra, then tore off her clothes, straddling one of my breasts while she rubbed her wet pussy over my erect nipple.

"Mmm," she purred. "There's *so* many ways to make love to your beautiful body."

"Oh yeah?" I grinned, suddenly forgetting all of my previous concerns and grabbing my breast between two hands, rubbing it sexily over her slippery vulva. "Do you like that? Do you like fucking my tits?"

"Yes, I do," she moaned, looking at me with a Cheshire Cat grin. "But do you know what I'd enjoy fucking even *more*? Your beautiful face, and those puffy rosebuds lips."

"Mmm," I said, pulling her hips higher up on me until they covered my face. "Sit on my face, Liz. I want to watch you writhe and moan while I eat your pussy."

"*Fuck*, yes," Liz groaned, lowering her dripping pussy onto my lips. "Suck my cunt like you enjoyed that crème brûlée."

"Mmm," I purred. "You're *much* more moist and tasty than the President's favorite dessert."

"Yes, she *is*, isn't she?" a deep baritone voice suddenly said from the other end of the Lincoln Bedroom.

We both jerked our heads to see the President standing in the open doorway with his hands on his hips.

"I *knew* you two had something more going on ever since you both ducked out in the middle of the Correspondent's Dinner."

"James," Liz said, bending over to cover up my exposed body and pulling the sheets overtop the two of us. "I thought you had an important meeting?"

"What could be more important than watching my wife sit atop of a beautiful woman's face, moaning in delight?"

"You mean—you're not *angry*?"

"Are you *kidding* me?" he said. "I'm just thrilled that my wife has found a way to reignite her passion, even if it *is* with another woman. Besides, you know this is every man's fantasy..."

Liz peered at me under the covers, shaking her head in dismay.

"I'm sorry to put you in this predicament, Jade," she whispered. "I'll get dressed and get him out of here so you can have a little privacy."

"It's not a problem, really" I said, smiling at her under the covers. "It's not like I haven't been in this situation before. Why don't we make the most of it and have a little fun now that the opportunity presents itself?"

"Your mean—you don't mind playing it *both ways* sometimes?" she said.

"If the right man presents himself," I grinned, "I never pass up the opportunity to mix it up. And this man is certainly one in a million."

"What did you have in mind, exactly?" Liz asked.

"Why don't we give him a little show to start with? See if we can rev up his engines and rekindle some of that passion you say has been missing from your marriage all these years?"

"You're a *very* naughty girl," Liz said, giving me a huge smile.

"What do you say, dear?" the President said from the other side of the room. "Are you two going to have all the fun under the covers, or were you thinking of sharing in the spoils?"

Liz flew the sheets back toward the end of the bed and turned around to face her husband.

"Why don't you just sit down and *watch* for a little while?" she said. "I'd like to give you a little lesson in self-control for a change."

"Can I—um—at least *enjoy* myself while I watch?" the President said.

"No," Liz smiled. "I'd like to take a turn at being the Commander-in-Chief for a change. You're just going to have to sit there and squirm while the rest of the world revolves around *you* this time."

"If you *insist*," the President said, scrunching down in one of the old armchairs and spreading his legs with a huge bulge in his pants.

"What do you say, Jade?" Liz purred. "Shall we pick up where we left off?"

"By all means," I said, grasping the sides of her ass as she lowered her pussy back down onto my face.

But this time, Liz leaned forward over my head and rested her elbows on the pillows above me, giving her husband a wide-open view of her exposed ass and vulva grinding against my chin.

"Oh my God," the President groaned as he watched his wife roll her hips on my face and moan in delight.

"Does that turn you on, babe?" Liz said. "Do you like watching your wife getting eaten out by a beautiful woman?"

"*God* yes," he said, unzipping his fly.

"No *touching*, remember?" Liz said, grinding her snatch into my face as her juices began streaming down over my chin and my neck.

"I promise," he said. "I'm just freeing the beast. Otherwise, I might rip a hole in my pants from how hard you're making me right now."

"*Good*," Liz said. "Enjoy the show. Maybe you can pick up some pointers."

For the next two or three minutes, Liz proceeded to grind her pussy into my eager mouth while I danced my tongue over her clit and the President hummed and groaned in delicious torture from the other side of the room. For some reason, I didn't mind him seeing my exposed breasts exposed behind Liz's bare bottom—it just added to the eroticism of the moment. Before long, Liz began to shake her hips more vigorously against my face, and I sucked her clit deep into my mouth knowing she was getting close to reaching her climax.

When it finally hit her, she squealed out loud while I watched her tits bouncing and shaking above me in the throes of ecstasy. I cupped her ass tightly in my hands until I felt her buttocks stop shaking, then she lifted her leg and turned around to face the President. When we both looked in his direction, we saw that he'd pulled his pants all the way down to his ankles with his erection flapping up excitedly against his abdomen and a small stream of pre-cum dribbling down the underside toward his tight balls.

His cock was larger than most, perhaps eight inches long with a perfectly straight shaft and a large, glistening circumcised crown. He looked at the two of us with lust in his eyes, gripping the arms of the Victorian chair so tightly his knuckles were blue.

"My oh my, James," Liz teased. "I haven't seen you in such a state of excitement in years. Maybe we should invite an extra paramour into our bedroom more often. You look like you could pop off any second."

"It's taking every ounce of my strength not to pounce on top of the two of you right now," he said. "This is torture watching you."

"Good," Liz scoffed. "Now you have a sense what it's been like being neglected all these years. I want you to see what it's like on the other side of the coin for a change. You just continue sitting there for a little longer while Jade and I have some more fun."

"Liz..." the President protested. "You can't leave me hanging like this–"

"Oh, I can, and I *will*. Just pretend you're sitting in the Situation Room with all your military advisors while you watch helplessly as the North Koreans taunt you with repeated missile launches over the North China sea. *I'm* the one in control, this time, dear."

"You're evil, you witch," he groaned.

"You have *no* idea," Liz smiled. "Jade, do you mind if I *watch* my husband suffer this time while we have some more fun?"

"Whatever you say, boss," I smiled. "I'm just enjoying watching you two build the sexual tension."

"May I remove the rest of your clothes?" she said, winking at me.

"We're in this pretty deep already," I smiled. "Knock yourself out."

Liz leaned over and unbuckled my belt then pulled my dress pants and panties down over my feet and threw them on the adjacent settee. Then she pressed my thighs upward in the same way I'd done with her earlier at the hotel, but this time she turned around and lowered her ass onto my pussy facing toward the President, in the reverse cowgirl position. With both of our legs splayed wide apart mere inches away from the President's ogling eyes, he could clearly see our dripping pussies touching and rubbing against one another.

Liz leaned forward slightly then arched her back as our engorged glands touched, and we both moaned in pleasure. I could hear the President groan also, and I could only imagine what kind of pain he was suffering not being able to join us or touch himself. As Liz began to slide her wet pussy over mine and moan in delight, she continued to taunt and torment her husband.

"Do you *like* seeing our wet pussies rubbing together, James?"

"God, yes," he grunted.

"Do you wish your cock was wedged between these two beautiful cunnies while we soaked you with our juices?"

"*Fuck*, yes," he groaned.

"Would you like to bury your big dick in my snatch while Jade's tribbing my hard clit?"

"Oh God, Liz," he whinnied. "You have no idea."

"I can see you dripping all the way down that big pole and over your beautiful balls," she said.

"*Please*, Liz," he pleaded. "Let me *touch* myself at least. You're killing me."

"I want this to be a lesson to you," she said. "About the power of a passionate, emotional connection. Like the one every husband and wife should share."

"Yes, Liz," the President nodded.

"Like the one every husband and wife should savor together..."

"Yes, baby," he panted.

"Do you want to watch me cum all over Jade's pretty pussy?"

"God, yes. Let it go, baby. Come for me while I watch your beautiful body shaking and quivering in ecstasy."

"Are you ready to cum with me, Jade?" Liz said, turning her head halfway around to peer at me.

"Damn straight, girl," I moaned, feeling my own climax barreling toward me like a freight train.

"Okay, Jade," Liz's voice squeaked, suddenly rising in volume. "I'm going to cum. Let me see you gush all over my twat. I'm cumming, baby!"

I grabbed the sides of Liz's ass and curled my pelvis up toward her hole, feeling the insides of my pussy beginning to throb and contract tightly. As Liz wailed at the top of her lungs in delirious ecstasy, I gushed hard jets of fluid against her pulsing vulva while my anus snapped open and shut mere inches away from her apoplectic husband. While the two of us bucked and screamed in orgasmic union, I could have sworn I heard the sound of slapping skin coming from the President's chair.

When Liz and I finally came down from our highs, Liz lifted herself off me and kissed each of my breasts before giving me a peck on the cheek. Then she lifted up both of our bras lying beside us on the bed and slowly ambled over to the President's chair.

"You've been a *very* bad boy, Mr. President," she said, noticing him holding his purple pecker in both of his hands tightly. "I told you no touching. I'm afraid we're going to have to take more drastic measures now."

As the President looked at her sheepishly, she pulled his hands off his dripping cock and forced them behind the back of his chair, tying them tightly to the backrest with the two bra straps. When he was sufficiently immobilized, she walked around in front of him and slapped her tits across his face, making them redden.

"You don't *look* like the most powerful man in the world now," she teased. "How does it feel to be subjugated and controlled by the whims of a distracted partner?"

"Not so bad, actually," he smiled. "I could kind of get used to this."

"That's not what your *little* head seems to be saying," she said, noticing the streams of precum cascading down both sides of his engorged cock like a waterfall. "Don't you want to feel my warm, slippery pussy taking your big thumper inside me?"

"Yes, please Liz," he pleaded. "I want to feel you inside. I want to make love to you so bad right now."

"What do you think, Jade?" Liz said, smiling over at me. "Should I put him out of his misery, or are you enjoying this show too much?"

"Maybe just a little bit longer," I teased. "We don't want him to forget what it takes to please a woman and who's in charge now."

"You little–" the President started.

"*Uh, Uh!*" Liz shook her head, chiding him. "That's my new best friend you're talking about. From now on, *I'm* the one calling the shots as to what happens to her and what kind of role she's going to play in our campaign. Is that clear?"

"Yes, dear," the President groveled. "I'll do anything to reconnect with you. I just want to feel your beautiful, warm body next to me."

"That can be arranged," Liz said while circling around him, shimmying her ass mere inches away from the tip of his cock.

"Do you promise to love me, and hold me, and cherish me for the rest of our days?" she said.

"Yes, Liz. I've always loved you. I just never gave you the attention you deserved."

"Do you promise to tuck me in every night with a sweet bedtime kiss?"

"Yes, baby."

"And make love to me whenever either one of us feels the urge?"

"Oh *God* yes," the President panted, staring between Liz's legs at her glistening gap while she bent over him, tantalizing inches away from his throbbing crown.

"Even if North Korea or China have just declared war on the U.S.?"

"Um..."

"I'm *kidding*, you big brute," Liz said as she finally placed her dripping slit over his pulsing member and slowly slid herself down his shaft.

"Oh my God, Liz," the President groaned. "You've never felt so good..."

"Is that just because you're all turned on from watching me make love to Jade?"

"No, it's because I've never felt this close to you. Now I finally recognize how important you are to me. I'll never neglect you again."

"Okay, baby," Liz smiled. "I believe you. Now fuck me with that big

President Johnson and let me feel you squirting inside me. I'm going to come again."

"Yes, Liz," the President groaned. "I'm going to come for you. I'm going to come like I've never come before in my whole life. Squeeze my cock while I come inside you."

While the President unleashed a howl of pleasure, Liz grabbed the two sides of the armrests and threw her head back in ecstasy while her pussy clamped down on the President's cock. I watched the two of them rocking and thrashing their hips together while the base of the President's dick pulsed in a series of powerful surges as he emptied his seed inside her.

I wasn't sure what my future would be in their administration, but there was one thing I was certain of at this moment. The President would no longer take his wife for granted again, and their bond would forever be unbreakable from this moment forward.

VOLUME FOUR

THE COSTUME PARTY

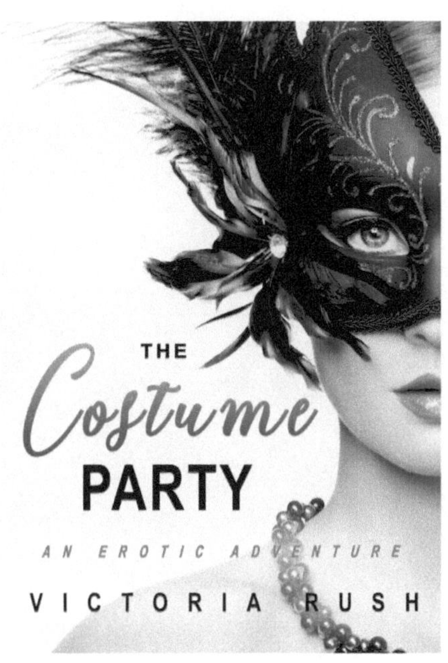

1
———

I woke up to the sound of my best friend Hannah calling me from the other end of my house. She'd let herself in early on a Saturday morning and for some reason was yelling at me as she ran up the stairs.

"Jade!" she hollered. "Where are you? I've got some exciting news!"

I rolled over and squinted at my clock on the nightstand. It was a little past eight. Saturdays were the only day of the week I allowed myself to sleep in, and I was more than a little ticked at her rude intrusion.

"Aren't you up yet?" she called. "Get up—you're not going to believe what I just heard."

I rolled over and wrapped my pillow around my ears as she dashed into my bedroom. She paused for a minute smiling at my feeble attempt to block her out of my morning daze, then she pounced on the bed below my curled-up knees.

"Wake up, sleepyhead!" she squealed, pushing my shoulders to rouse me from my slumber.

"This better be good," I said, raising my pillow a few inches and peering at her through thin eyes. "You know how much I worship my weekend sleep-ins."

"You'll be glad I woke you when you hear what I have to tell you," she said. "Besides, you're gonna want to get up and begin planning your day right away. We're going to need a few extra hours to go shopping."

I pulled my duvet cover over my shoulders and huffed.

"What could possibly be so important to drag me out of my soft and cozy bed this early in the morning?"

I peered outside, looking at the gray clouds hanging low in the late October skies. I was in no hurry to venture out into the chilly autumn air.

"Only the biggest private shindig of the year. Steve Bannon is hosting his annual Halloween party at his mansion on the lake, and we're invited!"

"Isn't that the party with all the A-list celebrities? How did you score an invitation?"

Hannah peered at me with a wicked look in her eyes.

"Let's just say I know somebody who knows somebody. Someone with whom I may have pulled a few strings to earn some special favors."

"I bet that's not the *only* thing you were pulling to earn those favors," I said, raising an eyebrow.

"Possibly," she smirked. "But I apparently impressed him enough with my naked gymnastics to land an invitation to this special event. Except this year, it's got an extra twist. This time it's going to be a *nude* costume party."

I lifted my head and propped the side of my face on a crooked elbow, suddenly intrigued.

"Isn't that an oxymoron? How can you be in costume and naked at the same time?"

Hannah smiled and handed me a gold-embossed card inscribed with fancy calligraphy writing. I felt the raised surface of the script on the tips of fingers, rubbing it gently trying to divine its meaning through my still bleary eyes. Somebody had gone to a great deal of effort to create an invitation card on par with the most extravagant wedding.

I pulled myself up and leaned against my headboard, slowly reading the message.

You are cordially invited to attend my annual Halloween costume ball at my estate overlooking Lake Michigan.

This year I've added a special twist to make it even more interesting. You're encouraged to wear as little or as much trappings as you feel comfortable—including nothing at all beyond a simple mask. With everyone baring a little more than usual, who knows what kind of shenanigans might break out, and we're always mindful of protecting the anonymity of our special guests.

Of course, I encourage everyone to be playful and creative with their choice of costumes, as this is always the highlight of the event. As in previous years, there will be a special prize for the best costume of the evening and we hope you'll be suitably daring and inventive.

Feel free to bring a partner and let down your britches! As always, what happens at the Bannon residence stays at the Bannon residence. I look forward to seeing you this Saturday, starting at midnight. We'll all have a ghoulish good time!

I peered up at Hannah and grinned.
"No RSVP?"
"There's no need with a Steve Bannon invitation," she said. Everyone who's invited always goes. It's the go-to event of the year in the Chicago area. Models, actresses, rock stars, billionaires—everybody who's anybody in this town will be there. There's even a rumor that the Governor and his wife will attend this year's event."
I looked down at the card, rubbing my fingers over the embossed script.
"The invitation says you're allowed to bring a partner. Was that a condition of your little tryst with your friend—that you accompany him as his plus-one?"
Hannah peered at me devilishly as a tiny curl formed on the sides of her mouth.
"When I told him I had a friend who was even prettier than me

and had a body to die for, he didn't hesitate to hand me an extra invitation. *You're* my plus-one, girl." She pulled another card out of her purse and handed it to me. "You know I'd never pass up an opportunity like this without bringing my bestie along to share in the fun."

I looked at Hannah with a quizzical look and shook my head in confusion.

"How are we ever going to find a decent Halloween costume on the Saturday before the end of the month? All the costume stores will be sold out of the best stuff."

Hannah kicked off her shoes and lifted the covers, then scooched in excitedly next to me against the headboard.

"I've been searching online for some ideas. We don't have to wear anything too elaborate, and there's no reason why we have to stick to a Halloween theme. Remember, this is a *nude* costume party. We already look pretty hot for a couple of girls nearing middle age. The less we wear, the better. Let's flaunt it while we've still got it!"

She pulled an iPad out of her purse and tapped the screen. A website opened showing a collection of sexy models wearing risqué costumes. She scrolled through the images, commenting on the various themes.

"Just look at some of these possibilities. We can play any role we like, wearing as much or as little as we please. Most of these costumes can be put together with a simple trip to Walmart and maybe a bit of needle and thread. Plus, we can easily remove one of two pieces from each outfit to reveal a bit more skin. The most important element is the headpiece. We just need something to conceal our identity and highlight our girly figures with a bit of flair."

Hannah paused at a picture of a sexy blonde wearing a Playboy bunny costume. She wore a tight corset and a rubber mask that covered the top half of her face with tall ears pointing up in the air.

"What about this one? You have to admit, it's pretty hot. You'd could even dispense with the bodice altogether and just keep the bunny tail on your naked ass. Imagine the looks you'd get prancing around his mansion in that costume!"

The images of sexy half-nude models wearing unusual masks

reminded me of my encounter at the Fantasy Feast naked dinner party. Suddenly, I became mindful of the wetness that had begun building between my legs.

"Not bad," I said, shifting my weight uncomfortably off the wet spot on my sheets. "Show me some more."

Hannah flipped through a few more images and stopped at a picture of a sexy maid wearing a lacy dress, holding a feather duster in her hand. Her firm tits pressed against the flimsy fabric, creating an irresistible focal point from the sensuous shadows on her bosom.

"How about this?" she said. "You'd look stunning in this outfit. You'd be covering up just enough to drive every man and woman at that party absolutely crazy. And imagine all the fun you could have teasing the naked guests with your little duster!"

"Intriguing..." I said as I squeezed my thighs together, trying to quiet my burning clit.

The more images Hannah showed me, the more turned on I got. Whether it was from me imagining myself in the costumes or imagining myself playing with the guests dressed up in the provocative outfits, was unclear. Either way, the more my mind began to ponder the possibilities, the more excited I became about going to this event.

"The only problem is, it will be difficult to cover my face without looking unnatural in that outfit," I frowned. "Show me more costumes with masks."

Hannah refined her search by typing in the words *sexy mask costumes* and the screen refreshed showing a new set of models in racy outfits. Many of the themes revolved around superheroes, with the male models sporting Batman and Superman motifs and the female models wearing Wonder Woman and Batgirl-type costumes.

"Not very original," I frowned. "I bet there'll be a ton of superhero costumes among all those egotistical celebrities. I'm looking for something a little different."

Hannah paused for a moment, then tapped on her photo library pulling up an image of me wearing a business suit painted on my naked body.

"Remember that time you went to the nude bodypainting workshop? You're a graphic artist. You can be virtually anything you want and show off all you wish with a little bit of well-disguised paint. Whether it's Catwoman, Black Widow, or Wonder Woman–all these characters wear is a mask and tight outfits to show off their beautiful physiques. You could even dress up like Mystique in the X-Men movie and wear absolutely nothing other than a full coat of body paint."

"Been there, done that," I said. "If I'm going to really enjoy myself, I want to wear something I've never worn before that will absolutely blow everyone away."

"You sure are a tough customer," Hannah said, shaking her head. "Let's try something a little different..."

She reopened her browser and typed in the words *naked masquerade costumes*. A gallery of Google images popped up with a collection of half-naked men and women.

"*Now* we're talking," I said, squirming on the bed as I scanned the toned bodies of the sexy models.

"Look at that one," Hannah said, pointing at the screen. "It's a picture of Rihanna at last year's Met Gala dressed as Nefertiti. With her sheer lace dress and silver headdress, it doesn't leave much to the imagination. A bit more makeup around the eyes, and you'd be able to mask your identity quite easily."

"That's pretty hot," I said, beginning to feel the sheets getting wetter and wetter between my legs. "She definitely looks fuckable. But it's been done before. I don't want to wear something half of these people will have already seen."

"Damn, girl, you're *impossible!* Remember, less is more. The idea is to show as much of our bodies as possible to attract the attention of all these beautiful people. You could get away with a simple mask, a painted emblem on your chest, and a shiny belt. Who really cares what you're wearing as long as you get the attention of the guests?"

"Humor me for a little longer," I said, squeezing Hannah's leg. "I'm starting to get a few ideas. I just need a bit more inspiration."

Hannah began flipping through the images more quickly until one picture suddenly caught my attention.

"Wait!" I said. "Go back a few frames. I saw something

interesting..."

She scrolled back until an image of six men dressed in contrasting costumes popped up.

"That's the one," I said, scanning the image slowly.

"*The Village People*?" Hannah said. "That might be okay for a gay guy, but how could you possibly look sexy wearing any one of those cheesy costumes?"

My eyes darted back and forth between the sexy cowboy wearing chaps and the indian warrior wearing a feathered headdress and a skimpy loincloth. Suddenly I nodded as a mischievous smile formed on my face.

"What?" Hannah said. "What could you possibly be thinking?"

She glanced down at my breasts peeking above the covers, noticing my hardening nipples.

"Because I know gay dudes—even ones with hard bodies like these guys—don't do it for you. Where is your mind going with this idea?"

"I've decided what I'm going to wear," I said, crossing my arms over my chest. "But I'm going to keep it a secret until we get to the party. It'll be all the more fun and surprising if I reveal it at the last second. But I promise you, it'll be one-of-a-kind and extremely provocative."

Hannah's eyes darted across my face, trying to imagine what I had in mind.

"Now you've got *me* all excited thinking what you're going to do. Judging by your obvious state of arousal, your head is already at the party. Can I crawl under the covers with you and have some fun fantasizing which one of those costumes you're going to wear?"

"By all means," I said, disappearing under the covers with her. "Just imagine me as one of those hot dudes with his clothes off."

"Mmm," Hannah purred, slithering between my slippery thighs. "I'd rather imagine you as a hot *chick* with her clothes off."

"In a couple of days," I said, spreading my legs further apart and pulling her face into my steaming crotch. "You might be able to have it both ways."

2

Just after midnight on the day of the party, I pulled my car up beside a call box in front of a large wrought-iron gate protecting the entrance to Steve Bannon's estate. After providing our names and the identification numbers on the front of our invitation cards, the gates opened and we followed the curved driveway up to the front of a giant French-styled chateau. As a parking attendant approached our car, I turned to Hannah seated next to me and smiled.

"It's show time," I said.

"Not a moment too soon," she huffed. "I've been dying to see what you're wearing under that coat ever since you picked me up."

I'd intentionally worn a long western duster to cover my body all the way from my shoulders to my ankles. Part of it was meant to surprise Hannah when I finally reached the event, but it had much more to do with my desire to shock everyone else once I got in the front door. I reached behind my seat and pulled a thin black mask out of a bag on the floor and wrapped it around the top of my face.

Hannah's forehead wrinkled as she looked at me, still confused.

"Let me guess: Kato, Zorro, Nightshade?"

"You're moving in the right direction with the first two," I smiled, reaching back into the bag and pulling out a pair of western boots.

"Cowboy boots?" Hannah squinted. "I don't know my cowboy characters quite as well—"

"Maybe this will help," I said, donning a white Stetson.

Hannah looked at me blankly for a moment, then her eyes lit up, recognizing the familiar image of the famous cowboy with the white hat and black mask.

"The Lone Ranger?"

"Yes, but with a little twist. You'll have to wait for the full reveal until we get inside."

"You're such a tease," she said as I handed the attendant my keys and we stepped out of the car.

We paused for a moment, taking in the full scale of the Bannon estate close-up. The four-story mansion extended almost a hundred feet in either direction, with tall arched windows and ornate brick-work. The bright spotlights illuminating the front of the house lit up the entire courtyard, reflecting off Hannah's shiny Batgirl outfit.

"Holy shit!" she exclaimed. "This place is gigantic. We're going to have to drop *breadcrumbs* to not get lost in there."

"More like *caviar* or *foie gras*," I chuckled. "Something tells me everything about this affair is going to be top shelf."

"What are we waiting for?" Hannah giggled, rushing ahead of me toward the front door.

My gaze drifted down while I soaked up her tight ass in her black latex outfit. She had a beautiful hourglass figure, and the tight Batgirl costume highlighted every curve of her sexy body. I smiled as I imagined the two of us mingling among the high rollers. But I had a feeling they'd be focused on someone *else's* ass tonight.

With the large double entrance doors pulled back, we peered into the bright marble-floored foyer as we approached the front steps. A large crowd of costumed guests had already begun to gather in the main ballroom, and we could hear soft jazz music wafting out into the courtyard.

"Good evening ladies," a man wearing a crisply tailored tailcoat and black tie said as we stepped into the entrance hall.

He looked at my long shawl and smiled.

"May I check your coat, Madam?"

"Yes, thank you," I said, turning my back to assist him in its removal.

When he pulled the cape off my back and viewed my naked backside, I heard him gasp. To complement my Lone Ranger disguise, I'd chosen to wear a tight-fitting black leather vest and long black chaps with nothing underneath. My tight ass poked out the back of the open leggings, and I could feel him running his eyes up and down my body as he hesitated hanging my coat in the closet.

But when I turned around, both Hannah and the doorman took a step back in shock. On the front of my open pants, I wore a large dildo fashioned in the shape of a man's cock and balls, framed by two silver pistols on either side of my hips. The long phallus slapped against the sides of my naked thighs as it swung from side to side.

"Holy *fuck*, Jade!" Hannah squealed. "That's *outrageous*! Where did you ever come up with that idea?"

"Remember the Village People picture you showed me a few days ago? I decided to borrow elements of both the cowboy and the indian characters to create my own design." I shook my hips to juggle my equipment and smiled. "I thought it would be kind of fun playing *both* sides of coin, so to speak."

"Uh—*yeah*," she said, flicking her eyes between my tight bosom spilling over the top of my vest and my faux genitals. "I'd have to say you pulled it off. With that getup, I expect you'll be the center of attention all night long."

"Um," the doorman said, shyly interrupting. "May I have your tickets, please?"

"Of course," I said, rustling my rubber balls as I fished in the pocket of my chaps for my ticket. When the butler turned to collect Hannah's ticket, I could see the front of his pants tenting in obvious arousal.

"Enjoy your evening," he said, motioning for us to enter the ballroom.

"Oh, I have a feeling we will," Hannah winked, as she nodded toward the lengthening pole pushing down his pant leg.

A waiter approached us with tall glasses of champagne on a silver tray and did a double-take when he noticed the swinging package between my legs.

"Whoa boy," Hannah said to the server, taking two glasses off his unsteady tray. "We wouldn't want you to spill your load before we've sampled the goods."

As we moved into the main entrance hall, the patrons milling in small groups began to turn around to view the newly arriving guests. Suddenly, the gentle buzz of group conversation receded until the only sound we could hear was the hum of the background music. Everyone was so stunned taking in my outfit, they were literally dumbstruck with their mouths agape.

Many of the guests had chosen to wear predictable Halloween costumes with little bits of flesh showing here and there, but nobody was letting it all hang out quite as brazenly as I had. Amid the predictable sprinkling of ghosts and goblins, there was a profusion of superhero figures and Disney characters bedecked in various stages of undress. I shook my head at the lack of imagination of the high-powered group and began to wonder if the event was going to live up to Hannah's hyperbole.

"Damn, girl," she said. "It looks like you're going to be this evening's scene-stealer. You've already stopped the show. I don't know what everybody's thinking right now, but that thing looks so realistic, they must be wondering if you're a legit tranny wearing that impressive package."

I smiled a crooked grin, suddenly feeling self-conscious with all of the eyes in the room surveying my exposed body. Fortunately, a handsome couple dressed as Anthony and Cleopatra began to approach us, providing some distraction.

"Welcome to our little costume party," the man said, extending his hand to Hannah and me. "I'm Steve Bannon and this is my wife

Genevieve. You'll have to excuse me, but I don't recognize either of you under your—*interesting* disguises."

I was taken aback by how handsome the eccentric billionaire looked close up. With his square jaw, dimpled cheeks and thick head of salt-and-pepper hair swept back in a dense poof, he looked like a slightly older version of the famous actor Patrick Dempsey. He wore a loose toga draped over his well-muscled chest, and I could see his pecs flexing as he shook my hand.

But I found his wife even more beguiling. Wearing a tight-fitting gold-lamé dress slitted at one side of her hips and a pretty beaded headdress, she looked like a dead-ringer for a young Elizabeth Taylor. As I ran my eyes shamelessly over her luscious figure, I felt a sudden dampness building under the weight of my latex balls pressing against my flaring clit.

"Jade," I introduced myself, not yet wanting to reveal my full identity.

"Hannah," my partner responded, politely shaking their hands.

"It appears that you two have already captured the attention of my guests," Bannon said, turning to appraise the congregation still gazing awkwardly in our direction. He extended his arm in the direction of the main hall and nodded. "Please, come in and mingle. There are so many fascinating people to meet. I'm sure we'll catch up with the two of you a little later this evening."

"I'll look forward to that," I said, smiling at Genevieve, lingering for a moment longer at her dazzling figure. She returned the gesture, widening her eyes as my member twitched while I held my palm over the handle of one of my six-shooters.

"Holy shit," Hannah said, as Bannon and his wife melted back into the crowd. "Did you see the way he was looking at you? He was practically *raping* you with his eyes. Something tells me this is going to be a very interesting night. It seems the men are even more enamored with your disguise than the women. Either there's a lot of bi-curious guys in here, or they're attracted to that whole futa thing."

"I dunno," I said. "I'm showing off a lot of *girl* parts too. Who's to say what they're more attracted to? But did you notice his wife? I'd far rather get into *her* pants."

"It's too bad that thing isn't animated," Hannah chuckled, glancing at my pendulous dick. "If you could actually get it up, you could probably have your way with just about everybody in this place."

"Who knows?" I said, winking at Hannah. "In my current state of arousal, I wouldn't be surprised if this thing had a life of its own."

Little did she know how much truth in this statement I was about to reveal before the evening was over.

3

After Bannon and his wife resumed mingling with the rest of the crowd, Hannah and I wandered into the main ballroom. At first, most of the assembled groups gave us a wide berth, unsure what to make of the two girls dressed in such revealing costumes. Hannah's latex Batgirl outfit clung to her naked body like a second skin, the shiny fabric accentuating every crease and curve like it was painted on her. And the cutouts on both sides of my leather chaps left little to the imagination, even with the modicum of cover provided by my fake genitals covering my bare mound.

I was glad to have the freedom to mill about the room for a while, surveying the faces and costumes of the high-powered gathering. I recognized a fair number of public figures from the senior ranks of the local political, business, and media fields. The mayor was there with his wife, dressed as Little Red Riding Hood and the Big Bad Wolf, which seemed fitting given the ongoing level of corruption at City Hall. Bannon's business partner and fellow billionaire Kent Schiffer circled the room with a familiar supermodel, outfitted in matching red tights as Mr. Incredible and Elastagirl. And our local news anchorman was paired with his pretty sidekick, dressed as Woody and Bo Peep from the movie Toy Story.

Many of the guests were dressed as famous characters from superhero movies or nursery rhyme stories, with most of the men playing the more dominant role. *Typical display of macho-entitled privilege,* I thought. *Why does it seem every man who achieves a certain degree of power have to lord it over everyone else, thinking they're better than the rest of us?* My cheeky cowboy costume seemed a perfect counterpoint to the heavy dose of testosterone permeating the room, mocking their oversize male egos as I swung my big dick around like I owned it.

As Hannah and I began mingling with the small cliques scattered around the room, I found it amusing that while most of the women praised my cocky outfit, their male partners seemed threatened by it, silently stealing glances at my huge dong while their wives and girl-friends chatted with me comfortably. I wasn't sure if it was because they felt intimidated by my outsize genitals, or because they were secretly fantasizing about fucking me.

As more and more people began gravitating toward us, intrigued by my outrageous costume, Hannah slowly drifted off to the other side of the room. I couldn't blame her, with everyone asking me silly questions like what it felt like to be a woman carrying a man's dick. For a while I amused them, swinging my hips from side to side and playfully grabbing my balls, flaunting my male persona.

But I soon tired of the incessant stares and never-ending quips about my tranny disguise, and began looking for an excuse to break away. Just as I was about to excuse myself to go to the ladies' room, the governor and his wife approached our group and introduced themselves. They were dressed in matching his and hers chef outfits, the only difference being that his wife wore a less poofy hat and a backless apron that showed off her sexy ass and legs.

"That's quite a provocative costume," the governor said, extending his hand to me. "I'm Jack Scanlon and this is my wife, Alicia."

"Pleased to meet you, Mr. Governor," I said, quickly seeing through his thin disguise. "But no less daring than your wife's, which I dare say is even *more* revealing."

"In some respects, possibly," he said. "Except you're revealing both sides of the coin."

"Heads *and* tails, you mean?" I smiled.

"In a manner of speaking," he said, temporarily at a loss for words by my sassy attitude. "Are you here alone tonight?"

I scanned the room and noticed Hannah chatting it up with a hunky guest dressed in a Tarzan outfit.

"It seems my partner is out looking for greener pastures. I guess she felt this one had been fully tilled."

"Oh?" the governor said, glancing at my pendulous prick. "Who's been doing most of the figurative plowing—you, or all these other farm animals?"

"At this point, I'd say everybody's just getting the lay of the land," I said, dragging out the metaphor. "Surveying the landscape, deciding the best place to position their hoes."

"I see what you mean," the governor said, his eyes widening from my double entendre. "You seem to be particularly–*ambidextrous* in that respect."

"I'm just having fun pretending what it might be like to cultivate both sides of the field," I said, running my eyes up and down his wife's sexy body before locking eyes with her. "You never know when a particularly fertile plot might need tending."

"Well put, my lady."

"Please—call me Jade," I said, turning my attention to his wife, who'd been staring at my outfit the entire time. "What about you, Alicia? Have you been enjoying the evening so far?"

"Yes," she said, happy to deflect attention away from her overbearing husband for a moment. "So many interesting people and costumes."

"I find yours very alluring also," I said, staring at her plump breasts pressing against the front of her skimpy apron. "But it seems that all your fun parts are hidden from view, at least while we're talking face-to-face. It's only when you turn around that you reveal your adventurous side."

"I guess you'll just have to catch me when my back is turned then," she said, winking at me sexily.

"I'll definitely be keeping a lookout. Hopefully we can catch up later."

As much as I wanted to continue our playful flirtation, I knew I'd never have a chance for some alone time with her as long as I continued to engage them as a couple. Besides, I was getting tired of her husband's thinly veiled sexist comments.

"Will you excuse me for a moment while I use the restroom?"

"Of course," she said. "But be careful in there. It's not as simple for us ladies to pee standing up as it is for the men."

"Not to worry," I smiled. "Fortunately, this thing is easily removed. Though it might be kind of fun to try it just once."

"Will you be using the men's or the ladies' room?" the governor smirked.

"I'm pretty sure the toilets are unisex in this place," I said, gently admonishing him for another chauvinist remark. "Which will be a refreshing change from the usually cramped ladies' rooms we have to endure in other public places. Enjoy your evening. Perhaps we'll see each other a little later."

"We'll look forward to that," the governor smiled.

As I pulled away from the crowd, I shook my head at the impudent tone of the governor, ignoring his beautiful wife while he shamelessly flirted with me. Little did he know that I was far more impressed with Alicia than by the trappings of his high political office. I felt like I needed to wash myself off after dealing with his sexist attitude and while looking for a place to freshen up, I recognized the familiar red and white uniform of the mayor's wife as she waited outside the closed door of an adjacent anteroom. As I approached her from the side, I admired her shapely legs and full bosom pressing against her tight bodice. Her Little Red Riding Hood costume seemed the perfect outfit to highlight her youthful face and figure.

"You'd think we wouldn't have to wait to use a toilet in this place," I said, sauntering up next to her. "There must be at least twenty washrooms in this mansion."

"No doubt," she laughed. "But even in a place like this, with this many guests, unfortunately we ladies still have to wait to use the lavatory." She glanced down at my faux genitalia and smiled. "It's too bad they don't have his and hers toilets like in most public settings. With that getup, you'd probably get away with slipping into the men's room."

"Maybe," I said. "But I'd still have to pee sitting down. I'm just looking to freshen up anyway. I was hoping for a respite from all the overcharged testosterone out there."

"Tell me about it," she nodded. "I've been dealing with city politics from the other side for almost twenty years now. It's still very much an old-boys network in this business. Women are just treated as chattel, to be trotted out as eye candy whenever there's a public relations opportunity like this."

"That's partly why I wore this outfit," I admitted. "I thought it would be kind of fun to swing my own dick around all these heavy hitters at this posh event."

The washroom door suddenly swung open and a woman wearing a Victorian costume brushed past us, sneering at our haughty outfits.

"Judging by the heft of that thing," she said, "I'd say yours is the biggest one here by a large margin. Do you want to join me while I freshen up inside? It looks like the last thing you need right now is to stand outside alone while everybody wags their tongues at you."

"Thanks," I said. scurrying in behind her as we locked the door, giggling like two schoolgirls. "I'm Jade, by the way," I said stretching out my hand.

"Haley," she said, grasping my hand firmly as she smiled into my eyes.

As we leaned in to the doublewide mirror over the marble vanity to check our lipstick and mascara, I noticed Haley's gaze drifting lower to check out my package.

"You know, if it weren't for the straps holding that apparatus onto your hips, I'd swear that thing was real," she said. "It's so life-like. Even your *testicles* look authentic."

"The whole thing is made out of a special latex engineered to mimic real skin. With all the advances in artificial dolls these days, it's amazing what they can do with sex toys."

"Do you mind if I—*touch* it?" she asked.

"I thought you'd never ask."

As I stepped back from the vanity, Haley turned to face me, reaching her hand down to touch my artificial cock.

"My God," she said, squeezing it firmly. "It even *feels* like a real dick. If only it could get hard, I shudder to think how big it would be angry."

As she reached further down to cup my balls, her face came closer to mine, and we kissed. I pressed my tongue into her mouth and she reached lower still, running her fingers over my moist labia. I purred in pleasure, pressing my crotch harder into her hips. She hiked up her skirt, and I was pleasantly surprised to see that she was completely naked underneath. Recognizing my opportunity to have a little fun, I positioned my hand over my right pistol, gently pumping the trigger. Slowly, my synthetic cock began to fill with air and inflate between her legs.

"What the—" Haley gasped, pulling back to see what was happening. "You've got to be kidding me. You can *animate* that thing?"

"In a manner of speaking," I said. "You want to give it a try?"

"*Hell* yes!" she said. "I'm so horny right now, I could fuck just about anything. But first, let me take a closer look at what I'm working with."

As I smiled at her wickedly, I pumped my trigger harder until my organ rose to a full ten inches of erect flesh. Haley couldn't help herself as she fell to the floor and took my member into her mouth while she proceeded to give me a pretend blowjob. As I watched her stretch her lips around my thick pole, I placed my hands behind her head and imagined fucking her face like a man. Although I was being far gentler than most, it was fun fantasizing being in the man's role for a change, having my way with my muse.

"That's it," I purred. "Suck my big cock, baby. Squeeze my balls while I fuck your pretty face."

Without hesitating, Haley reached underneath me and began

rubbing my balls against my raging clit. The sensation was not unlike what I imagined a real man would be feeling as she stimulated my sex organ.

"Fuck, yes," I panted. "That feels good, Haley. I want to fuck you so bad."

Suddenly, she stood up and smiled at me.

"That makes *two* of us. I'm so turned-on, I could pop off any second."

She reached behind her, placing her hands on top of the vanity and lifted herself up onto the counter, hiking her skirt all the way up. I took one look at her glistening pussy and leaned in to kiss her passionately. She reached down and pointed my hard pecker toward her opening and when I pressed it into her, she gasped.

"Oh God, Jade," she groaned. "Your cock feels so good. Fill me up with your big dick. I want to feel your balls slapping against my pussy."

Her dirty talk got me even more worked up, and as I pressed my hips forward, she moaned loudly. As we began to grind our hips together, our tongues danced in each other's mouths. Haley flapped her thighs against me as I plowed in and out of her, grinding my clit against the underside of my rubbery balls. While we grunted and moaned with abandon, anybody who might have been waiting to use the restroom must have surely known what was going on inside. But neither one of us cared, lost in the moment by the rising feeling of ecstasy engulfing our joined bodies.

Suddenly, Haley wrapped her legs around my ass and pulled me even deeper inside her pussy.

"*Damn*, girl," she panted. "You're going to make me come with that big thumper of yours. Fill me up while I come all over your pretty pussy."

"Yes," I groaned. "I'm close too. I'm going to cum with you. God damn, I like fucking you."

"Here it comes," Haley moaned. "Take me over the edge."

I grabbed Haley's hips by both sides and pulled her strongly toward me, grinding my cock and balls as hard as I could against her while ramming my cock in and out of her sloshing pussy. Suddenly, a wave of passion rolled over me as my clit began pulsating against the underside of my faux balls.

"Oh God, Haley," I groaned. "Cum with me baby. Come all over my big dick."

"Yes!" Haley howled. "I can feel you pounding my G-spot. It feels soooo good!"

Suddenly, I felt Haley spraying all over my balls and mound as her pussy clenched down over my phallus while we ground our hips against one another. We moaned inside each other's mouths as we locked lips in a tight and passionate kiss. After what seemed like a full minute of shaking and convulsing in each other's arms, our breathing finally returned to normal, while we kissed with me still inside her.

"*Ahem*," a woman's voice called impatiently from outside the door, from someone waiting to use the facilities.

"I guess we'll have to vacate the premises," Haley smiled. "Though I could make love to you all night long."

"Same here," I said. "Let's clean up and get out of here. Maybe we can find a more private place to continue our fun."

While Haley pulled down her skirt and reapplied her smudged lipstick, I unfastened my appendage and washed it under the tap before reattaching it to my mound. When we finally got ourselves put back together, we opened the door and walked past a long line of stunned onlookers as their eyes widened in shock ogling my still-dripping, semi-hard cock.

4

I t didn't take long after Haley and I returned to the main ballroom for her husband to spot us. While we giggled amongst ourselves about the pretentious costumes of all the men in the room masking their tiny peckers, the mayor approached us with an angry scowl on his face.

"Where've you been?" he barked at Haley, his ruddy, pockmarked face making his wolf costume look all the more ridiculous. "I've been looking all over for you. There are a lot of prominent people I wanted to introduce you to."

"Jade and I were just freshening up. No need to get your knickers in a twist, dear."

"*Freshening up*?" he said, darting his eyes back and forth between Haley's face and my tumescent cock. "How long does that take? You must have been gone for at least a half hour!"

"Well, you know how we women are when we hang out in the ladies' room," she replied with a straight face. "There's no telling how long it might take to get ourselves put together in front of the mirror. You *do* want me to look pretty and proper for all your important friends, don't you?"

"I—suppose so," he stammered, distracted by my glistening

joystick. He grabbed Haley's hand, trying to drag her away from me. "Come, I want you to meet one of my biggest fundraisers, Kent Schiffer."

As he steered Haley toward a gathering in the center of the room, she looked back at me with an apologetic expression, mouthing the words *later*. Soon after, Hannah came up behind me and cupped one of my bare cheeks with her hand.

"What was *that* all about?" she said. "It looked like the Big Bad Wolf was about to bite off his wife's head."

"He might as well have," I huffed. "The way he was acting as if he owned her. All these upper-class snobs seem interested in is congratulating themselves around their buddies while showing off their arm candy."

"He did seem a little distracted by you," Hannah said, noticing Haley peering in my direction with a flushed face. "And he wasn't the *only* one. What kind of trouble did you get into with his wife? You've got a strange glow about you."

"Nothing much," I lied. "We were just freshening up in the ladies' room, looking for an escape from all the overbearing egos in this place."

Hannah looked at me suspiciously, pinching her eyebrows as she peered at my puffy appendage.

"Well, judging by the flush on your chest and the sweat dripping down your ass, I'd say you were up to a little more than just fixing your makeup. If I didn't know better, I'd swear even your *dick* looks more excited than usual."

"We may have been touching up a bit more than just our *faces*," I admitted. "We started admiring each other's costumes and one thing led to another..."

Hannah reached down and squeezed my tumescent dildo, then her eyes widened as her lips curled up into a knowing smile.

"Is it just my imagination, or does it seem a little *bigger* than when we first came in? You better be careful—you could poke somebody's eye out with that thing."

"That's not the only thing it's good for poking," I grinned.

"No way!" she said, stepping back in mock indignation. "You were *fucking* the mayor's wife in the washroom? Did he have any inkling?"

"I don't think so. But judging by how much noise we were making in there, I imagine it won't take long for word to spread around the room."

"Not to worry–just stick with me, girl," Hannah said, moving closer to protect me from everyone's disapproving glares. "If any of these jokers cause you any trouble, I'll give them a batkick to the groin."

"I doubt that'll be necessary," I sighed, catching Hannah's Tarzan friend stealing glances at me from the open bar on the other side of the room. "Most of the men in here seem reluctant to engage me in any kind of conversation, let alone actually approach me in this getup. I don't know if they're more threatened by my provocative outfit or they're just afraid to admit they're attracted to a pretty girl with a big cock."

I noticed Tarzan moving to the other side of the bar to get a clearer look at me. I found it strange that he seemed so focused on me after Hannah had spent so much time with him earlier. Unlike me, I knew she had a preference for men, and I suspected she was hoping to land a wealthy boyfriend at this event.

"What about you?" I said, shifting my position to deflect Tarzan's gaze. "What kind of trouble have you been getting up to around all these society types?"

"Not as much as I'd like," Hannah frowned. "I've found a few interesting candidates, but so far everybody's been politely keeping their dicks in their pants."

"Well, you know how it is. With all their extra ornamentation, it might be kind of hard to just whip it out. Most of these guys seem to have gone to great lengths to gussy themselves up with all this embellishment."

"I know what you mean," Hannah said, pulling her tight latex skin down uncomfortably under her crotch. "I guess I didn't give this costume as much forethought as I should have. I'm sweating like a pig under here. I have to dismantle the whole thing just to go pee."

"Not exactly conducive to pulling off a quickie in this place," I chuckled.

"Not as easily as you," she grumbled. "You don't have to remove a single stitch of clothing to get your freak on. All you have to do is find a willing accomplice and insert your magic wand."

With Hannah's back turned away from the bar, I saw Tarzan adjusting his equipment under the counter. His loincloth had begun pouching in front of his penis, and he seemed to be getting more and more aroused watching me.

"What about that hunky Tarzan character I saw you flirting with earlier?" I said, hoping to redirect his attention. "He seems worthy of a little deconstruction."

"It crossed my mind, believe me," Hannah said. "But he seemed more interested in talking about everyone else in the room. Either he's just here for the people watching, or he's gay. I mean, I'm still a *catch*, right? Who can resist a sexy chick in this tight outfit? I was practically throwing myself at him."

Tarzan turned away from me holding his hands in front of his crotch, trying to keep his rising member from making too obvious an appearance. Then he suddenly stood up and exited through a door next to the bar.

"He's probably just trying to keep up appearances," I said. "It's a pretty snooty affair, you have to admit. People would likely get their nose out of joint if they caught a couple getting too carried away in public."

"That's what *powder rooms* are for, right?" Hannah grinned.

"Speaking of, I gotta go pee for real this time. Catch up with you in a bit?"

"Sure," Hannah said. "Just try not to dip your dick anywhere it doesn't belong this time. There's no telling what kind of hullabaloo it might generate if one of these heavy hitters caught you getting it on again with another one of their wives."

"Don't worry," I smiled. "I'll be staying far away from the ladies this time."

As soon as I left Hannah, a flock of men suddenly converged on her, no longer threatened by the presence of her sexy androgynous partner. But I was happy for the distraction, because there was something about this Tarzan hunk I needed to check out. He was the first man I'd met at the ball who'd demonstrated any genuine interest in me, and I wanted to see which persona he was more attracted to.

I meandered through the crowd making small talk with some of the guests then I ordered a cocktail at the bar and slipped quietly out the same door I'd seen Tarzan use. It led to a large wine cellar, darkened and chilled to a frigid fifty degrees. I looked around the room, catching sight of Tarzan huddled between two kegs with his hand moving suspiciously between his legs.

I strolled over in his direction and smiled when I noticed his predicament. His cock was at full mast, flapping up over his flimsy loincloth, high up against his belly. I nodded when I saw how well hung he was, his organ standing a good eight inches in length and at least two inches thick.

"Aren't you a bit underdressed for this place?" I asked.

"I suppose so," he said in a shaky voice. "But I didn't know where else to go." He looked down at his crotch with a sheepish expression, vainly trying to cover up his erection. "It seems I'm having a bit of a wardrobe malfunction."

"Is *that* what you call it?" I said. "Can I offer some help? Provide a little body heat at least? You're shivering in that skimpy outfit."

"Maybe," he hesitated, peering down at my even bigger cock hanging down over my naked belly. "At least you can provide some cover if anyone else comes in here."

As if on cue, the door on the other side of the wine cellar opened, and a uniformed waiter entered the room, walking in our direction. He appeared to be looking for a particular bottle, but when he caught sight of the two of us, he stopped and did a double-take. Without pausing, I stepped closer to Tarzan and flung my arms around him, pretending to make out. It was just the cover he needed, and this was the perfect excuse to get a little closer. The waiter smiled as he nodded toward us, then collected his items and exited the room.

"Thanks," Tarzan said, pulling away awkwardly. "This is beyond embarrassing. I can't seem to make this thing go down and I have nothing to cover up with."

"I can't imagine why you'd *want* to," I said, running my fingers over his hard chest muscles. "With a body like this, you should be showing off as much of it as you can."

He glanced down at my full breasts pressing up against him in my tight leather vest.

"I hadn't counted on getting quite so—*aroused* at this event," he stuttered. "I thought I'd be able to keep it together around all these stiff necks. This has never happened to me before in a public place..."

"Not to worry," I said. "This little accident will stay between us. But if you don't mind my asking, may I ask what's gotten you so worked up? I saw you looking in my direction, and all of a sudden you wanted to hide."

"I'm sorry," he said, his face flushing like a teenager. "I just couldn't help staring at you. I find you incredibly sexy, and with so much of you hanging out for everyone to see, I guess I just had a visceral reaction."

"I understand," I said, darting my eyes over his handsome face, finding myself getting surprisingly turned by his shy demeanor. "But which *part* of me were you most attracted to? I'm hanging out on both sides."

"Both," he said, without hesitation. "You have a sexy body and you're absolutely stunning. But there's something especially alluring about a woman flaunting a man's genitals overtop their naked body. It's very—*ballsy* of you."

"You like *cocky* women, do you?" I said, leaning in towards him as I brushed my thick cock against his tight balls.

"In a manner of speaking," he huffed.

"Did you want to play with it?"

"May I?" he said. "I've never really touched another penis before..."

"You mean besides your *own*?" I kidded. "Is that what you were doing in here? Stroking it trying to make it go down before you went back into the ballroom?"

"I was so turned on, I didn't think there was any other way to get myself back together."

"Maybe I can help you with that," I smiled, reaching down and grasping his throbbing cock with my left hand. "Is this warming you up a little bit?"

"Yes," he panted, clutching my ass while he rocked his hips toward me, trying to create some much-needed friction against his throbbing hard-on. "But you've got goosebumps too. How can I help warm you up?"

I wasn't sure what he had in mind, but I wasn't interested in him fucking me in the usual manner. I'd long been fascinated seeing gay men play with themselves. I found one of the most erotic things was when they rubbed their erect cocks together. Something about the playful jousting of their erogenous parts always got me turned on.

"Well, we're both equipped with similar equipment," I said, raising an eyebrow. "I've always wondered what it would feel like to rub two cocks together..."

"Oh my God," Tarzan said. "I've fantasized about that too. But you're not exactly *functional* in the way most men are—"

"You might be surprised what this ladyboy is capable of," I grinned. "This little package comes equipped with a few extra features."

As I began stroking his hard-on, I squeezed the trigger of the pistol on my right hip, slowly inflating my rising pecker. Tarzan looked down and widened his eyes, seeing my love muscle inflating to its full ten inches. When it reached its maximum length, I placed it against the underside of his prick and began rocking my hips in tandem with his. Even though he was better endowed than most men, my giant phallus looked like an anaconda slithering up next to his garden snake. As the rubbery veins of my dildo rolled over the sensitive flesh on the tip of his rod, he shuddered and emitted a drop of dew out of his hole.

"Uhnnn," he groaned. "This is incredibly hot. I've always wondered what this would feel like, but to do it with such a sexy woman is a dream come true."

"You've always wanted to get it on with a *tranny*?" I smirked. "Well now you've got your wish."

I reached down and cupped my hands around both of our cocks and began humping him more vigorously. Tarzan groaned as he placed his hands against my chest, squeezing my breasts over my cowboy vest.

"Open it up," I nodded. "See what it's like to fuck a real ladyboy. I want to feel your hard pecs rubbing against my tits."

He didn't need any more encouragement as he fumbled with my buttons until he freed my boobs from their tight enclosure. When he saw my firm breasts bouncing on my chest, he circled them with his hands and pinched my nipples gently while I continued frotting our cocks together in my hands.

"Fucking hell," he said. "You are so hot. You are truly the woman of my dreams."

"And *man* also?" I smiled.

"Yes," he admitted. "I've long fantasized what it would be like to hold another man's penis in my hands."

"Why don't you take the driver's seat then?" I said, acknowledging his bisexual nature. "Let me admire the scenery for a while."

When I removed my hands, he placed his palms around our joined cocks and squeezed them together firmly. More precum oozed out of the head of his pole, and he moaned as he began to pick up the pace of his rocking motion. Neither one of us seemed interested in kissing, fixated on the appearance of our two big cocks frotting in and out of his hands. As he began to moan more loudly, I slapped my sweaty breasts against his hard chest. I could tell he was getting close to the point of no return, and I was eager to watch him cum with our cocks joined together.

"Yes, baby," I purred. "Let it come. Cum all over my big tits. Let me hear Tarzan's call of the wild."

Suddenly, he arched his back and thrust his dick as hard as he could against my organ, pressing his balls tightly against mine. My clit throbbed as he shot one giant geyser after another between my boobs, cumming all over the underside of his chin and face.

"Fuckkkk!" he growled with each spurt. "I'm cumming all over your cock. *Uhn, uhn, uhn!*"

With each throb and spasm, he grunted like a wild animal until he was fully spent. When he finally recovered his strength, he looked up at me with gratitude.

"Thank you," he said. "I needed that. You were even more magnificent than I imagined."

"Glad I could be of service," I said. "Now you should get yourself back in there. Somewhere out there is your *real* Jane, waiting for you to scoop her up and take her away to your jungle."

"What about you?" he said, looking at me confused.

"I'm still looking for my Jane, too," I smiled.

The whole time neither one of us had so much as touched lips. All either one of us wanted was a quickie in the wine cellar, where we could live out one of our mutual boy-on-boy fantasies. As Tarzan tucked his pecker back under his loincloth and staggered out of the cellar, I smiled.

That's one way to get it on with a man, I thought. I wondered what other fantasies awaited me before the night would be over.

5

After Tarzan left the wine cellar, I found a sink nearby and cleaned myself up, removing all the cum that he'd splattered over my dildo and chest. Feeling flushed and sweaty, I decided to catch some fresh air before going back into the main room. A side door from the cellar led onto an expansive terrace overlooking the lake. Standing alone in a corner of the balcony stood the governor's wife Alicia with her back toward me. Her arms rested on the stone railing as she puffed a cigarette, leaning over with her naked ass jutting out behind her backless apron. My pussy fluttered as I admired her shapely figure, feeling the moisture accumulating on my lips tingling in the cool autumn air.

Alicia had one of the most magnificent backsides I'd ever beheld. Her long, slender legs were taut and shapely like a professional dancer's and her ass was as tight and firm as a teenager. The rising moonlight reflecting off Lake Michigan shimmered between the space in her thighs, illuminating the dark pit under her mound. It was almost as if she were daring me to approach her and fuck her from behind.

I surveyed the rest of balcony and seeing that we were alone, I began tiptoeing toward her. It was a calm and cloudless night and the light of the full moon shone brightly over the Bannon estate, revealing the splendor of its manicured gardens. Amidst autumn-speckled trees and perfectly manicured flower beds, lay a geometric hedge maze accented with stone sculptures and a flowing water fountain.

I paused for a moment to breathe in the floral scent of the breeze wafting in from the shore. I couldn't imagine a more romantic setting for a private encounter with my pretty temptress. As I edged closer toward her, I stepped on a small pebble and it went skittering over the stone tiles in Alicia's direction. She cocked her head and turned slightly in my direction, then bent lower on the handrail, taking another puff of her cigarette. Whoever she imagined approaching her from behind only increased the boldness of her seductive pose.

Maybe being the wife of the most powerful figure in the state gave her the confidence to blow off any would-be interlopers. Or maybe she was just bored and looking for an anonymous fling to mix up her dull political life. Whatever the reason, her self-assured nature turned me on even more and as the glistening slit of her pussy came into focus, I felt the wetness from my own sex beginning to run down the insides of my thighs. When I came within a few feet of her, she stood up with her arms extended on the balustrade and blew a stream of smoke high in the air.

"Beautiful night, isn't it?" she said to no one in particular.

"Spectacular," I said. "The view is truly magnificent in this light."

"Mmm," she replied, oblivious to the identity of her midnight paramour. "Were you admiring the landscaping?"

"Among other things," I said, staring at her bald snatch. "Everything is so perfectly balanced and neatly trimmed. It really makes you want to pause and appreciate Mother Nature."

Alicia took a step back with one of her legs, arching her ass higher.

"It would be a shame just to *look* at it," she said, "Nature is meant to be immersed in, don't you think?"

"Absolutely," I said, taking a step closer, brushing my bare breasts against her chilly back. "You never know what you might find until you make contact."

"Like the way a woman's nipples pucker when it's cold?"

"Or when they brush against a soft surface," I replied.

"Or her lover's skin," she said

She pressed her ass further toward me and touched my protruding organ, then gasped and turned her head in my direction, checking it before we made eye contact.

"And sometimes—" she mused, recognizing the familiar shape of my leather chaps. "Nature has a way of *surprising* us with her wonderful diversity."

"Do like surprises?" I teased.

"In the right circumstances."

I reached under the front of her apron and squeezed her breasts, pressing my cock harder between her legs. She reached underneath and began stroking my dildo against her wet cleft.

"I particularly like the way nature has a way of adapting to its surroundings—" I said, beginning to inflate my rubber penis with my pistol trigger. "Like the way it expands and contracts to fill the void in any particular situation."

"Yes," Alicia panted, running her hand up and down my giant shaft. "I'd like you to fill *my* void."

By now, my inflatable penis had reached its maximum length and Alicia was busy rubbing the bulbous head against her inflamed clit.

"Fuck me, Jade," she said, dispensing with any further pretense. "I've been fantasizing about you banging me with your beautiful dick all night long."

"As have I," I panted, angling the tip into her dripping opening. "I've dreamt of pounding your beautiful ass from the moment we met."

"*Fuck* yes," she grunted, as I pressed myself inside her. "Pound me with your big cowboy dick. Let me feel your balls slapping up against me while you ride me."

As I began to hump her, I marveled at how enthralled all the guests seemed to be with my transgender persona—both male and female. Everyone seemed to want a piece of my girl-cock, no matter how they could get it. While I watched my drumstick pounding in and out of her hole, I had to admit it was kind of fun assuming the male role for a change. There was something strangely empowering about being connected to a man's cock, watching all these strangers bow to my made-up masculinity. As I grasped the sides of her hips and pulled her toward me, she moaned and gyrated her hips, holding on to the rail for support.

"God damn, girl," she hissed. "You feel so good inside me. I've never had a man fill me up quite this way before. I only wish you could cum inside me. I want to hear you get off with me."

There was something about the sight of my big phallus plowing into her tight little ass that was getting me especially worked up. Even though she wasn't providing direct stimulation to my lady parts, I could have come just watching the incredibly sexy scene that was unfolding before my eyes. But I'd been saving up one more special secret. I pressed a button on the inside of my handle and suddenly my balls began vibrating from a battery-operated motor embedded inside. As I pressed my scrotum against her underside, I was instantly taken to a whole new level of excitement.

"Holy shit!" she squealed. "That's *definitely* something no man has ever done to me. Grind your nuts against me, Jade. Trib me with your big fat balls."

"Fuck, yes," I growled, feeling the rising tide of ecstasy building within me.

I couldn't help smiling, acknowledging the multipurpose capability of my male equipment. Not too long ago I was frotting a man with my big firehose, and now I was tribbing a sexy woman with my vibrating balls. For a brief moment, I felt envious of a man's equipment, but as my pussy began throbbing and dripping over my strap-on apparatus, I became acutely aware of my true gender. I leaned forward and rubbed my tits against Alicia's back, pinching and rolling her nipples between my fingers.

"Can you feel my wetness, Alicia?" I panted. "Can you feel how much you're turning me on?"

She reached under my vibrating balls and inserted two fingers inside me, stroking the front of my G-spot.

"Yes," she grunted. "You feel exquisite. You're going to make me come soon. I want to feel you come with me."

"With every part of my body actively engaged in fucking her, I didn't need any further encouragement. Within seconds, a surge of energy coursed through me, as my pussy began clamping down over Alicia's fingers. At the same time, she hunched over and began shaking wildly as she gripped the railing with all her strength.

"Fuck, Jade!" she hissed. "I'm cumming! Pound my ass with your big dick. God, I'm cumming so hard!"

As the two of us grunted and shook in simultaneous orgasm with my buttocks clenching as I pressed my cock deep into her, I suddenly became conscious of the extra light that was being cast onto the terrace from the open windows of the ballroom. When we finally came down from our powerful climax, she turned around and gently kissed me.

"It seems we have an audience," she smiled, directing her eyes toward the adjacent wall.

I peered in the direction of the ballroom and noticed a giant crowd of onlookers staring out the windows with their eyes and mouths agape.

"Good," I said. "It's about time some of these snobs got a taste of the real world outside their sheltered cocoons. "Maybe this will open their minds about the natural order of things."

With that, I lifted Alicia up onto the stone abutment and spread her legs far apart, pressing my still buzzing cock back inside her.

"If they want a show, let's really give them a show."

6

———

After Alicia and I came a second time in full view of the crowd, we took a moment to compose ourselves then walked back into the main ballroom as if nothing had happened. Neither one of us seemed to care that virtually everyone was staring at us as they continued gossiping in their little cliques. I didn't even bother to refasten my leather vest or deflate my dildo as my breasts bounced freely on my bare chest in tandem with my turgid hard-on.

The two of us approached the bar and ordered matching margaritas then giggled amongst ourselves about the way everyone was trying not to stare as they talked amongst themselves. In spite of the fact that they pretended to carry on normal conversations, it was obvious that they were still highly aroused by our little tête-a-tête.

"I think Mr. Incredible is regretting his wardrobe choice right about now," Alicia chuckled, motioning toward the billionaire and his supermodel girlfriend.

I stole a glance in their direction and noticed Schiffer had a pronounced erection tenting the front of his tights.

"He's looking more like *Mr. Fantastic* with that cucumber wedged between his legs," I joked.

"And check out our favorite newscaster," she said. "It looks like Woody's popping a little Pinocchio of his own."

I peered at the anchorman and noticed him rearranging the front of his denims as a prominent bulge ran down one side of his pant legs.

"Ha," I chuckled. "I bet he's wishing he wore chaps like me."

I had to admit that I was enjoying the attention of all the powerful people in the room, particularly amongst the men who seemed especially attracted by my naked ladyboy costume.

"I don't know about *Jack* though," she said, furrowing her brow as her husband marched toward us with an angry expression on his face. "I have a feeling that his little willie will be even more shriveled than usual after watching you pound me with your big tool."

The governor stormed up to the bar and grabbed Alicia's hand, trying to ignore the pink pole jutting up from my lap.

"What is it, dear?" Alicia said, feigning surprise at her husband's indignation. "I was just enjoying a quiet drink with my new friend."

"That was hardly *quiet!*" he huffed, dragging her off her barstool. "Come on, it's time for us to go."

"But the party was just getting started," Alicia protested. "I was just starting to get warmed up."

The governor glanced down at my flaring joystick then glared at me.

"It looks like the two of you were getting more than just *warmed up.*"

"Oh, come on, Jack," Alicia said, trying to resist his advance. "We were just having a little fun. You said that you wanted me to get more comfortable around your political friends."

"Not *that* way!" he fumed. "You've made a fool out of me and embarrassed me in front of all my colleagues!"

Alicia tried to protest, but the governor pulled her away from the bar and stormed toward the entrance. After collecting their coats from the butler, they soon disappeared out the front door. Alarmed by the commotion, Hannah joined me at the bar and sat on Alicia's stool, taking a sip of her cocktail.

"Jesus, Jade," she said, slapping my dripping dildo. "You sure know how to rock the boat in these genteel affairs."

"That's not the *only* boat I was rocking around here," I said. "Were you watching the show like everybody else?"

"How could I miss it?" Hannah chuckled. "It only took one person to catch you fucking the governor's wife before the entire room joined in the spectacle. Not like they could have *ignored* it, with all the grunting and groaning the two of you were doing."

"I wasn't paying much attention. I was kind of lost in the moment."

"You sure looked like it," Hannah said. "I have to say, It was an incredible turn-on watching you fuck her from behind. I could actually see your buttocks shaking when you came." She glanced down at my swollen cock and shook her head. "How does that work, exactly? I thought you were kind of detached from that thing."

"Not as much as you might imagine," I smiled. "Touch my balls to see for yourself."

Hannah placed her hand over my rubber scrotum and I switched on the vibrator, then her eyes suddenly flung open.

"Holy shit!" she said. "That thing really *is* fully animated. What else can it do? Spurt out fake cum?"

"As much as I wish it could, no. But these two extra tricks seem to be providing all the entertainment I need."

"I'd say so, judging by how loud the two of you were howling out there on the balcony. I fact, I've got a little girly hard-on of my own thinking what that would feel like inside me. I don't suppose we could find our own private alcove for a little fun, could we? I'm so horny right now, this costume is practically glued onto my body."

I glanced around the room and noticed that everybody was staring at us with disapproving expressions.

"Why not?" I said. "After that last escapade, it looks like all bets are off. There's not much to hide any more at this point."

I took Hannah's hand and began heading in the direction of the wine cellar, but Steve Bannon and his wife stepped in front of us, smiling like Cheshire Cats.

"It appears you've been enjoying my party even more than I could have imagined," he smirked, peering at my dripping dildo. "You seem to have gotten a rise out of more than a few of our guests this evening. I'd have to say you win the prize for the most inventive costume."

"I have to admit, it's been far less of a stuffy affair than I imagined." I glanced at Genevieve, noticing the slit in the side of her dress looking even more pronounced than before, revealing her hip bone above her barely concealed pussy. "I've found the conversation very stimulating."

"So it would seem," he said, staring at my tumescent totem. "Would you like to join my wife and me for a little nightcap in our private lounge? We've been admiring you all night long and would love to continue the conversation."

"Hmm," I said, raising an eyebrow toward Hannah. "Do you mind if I bring my friend along? We were just about to explore some private time of our own."

Bannon leered at Hannah's costume then smiled at her.

"I don't see why not," he said. "What do you think dear? Would you like to bring another partner into our little meeting?"

"The more the merrier," she smiled, jumping at the chance to have some more alone time with me. "Besides, now it'll be more evenly balanced. I'm not sure I could manage the two of you all by myself."

"Come then," Bannon said, leading us to a private elevator at the base of his stairs.

As we crossed the ballroom floor, the entire room followed our movement while my protruding penis waggled playfully between my legs. When we got in the elevator and the doors closed behind us, Bannon pressed button number four and smiled at Hannah and me.

"You've already explored many of the rooms in my house," he said. "But I think you'll find the view particularly appealing from the top floor."

I glanced toward Hannah and saw that her pupils were already dilated in excitement. I didn't know if she was more impressed by the fact that Bannon's mansion had four floors and a personal elevator or that she was about to participate in a private orgy with the richest man in the Midwest.

When the lift stopped and the doors opened, we both gasped at the view. The elevator opened to an enormous bedroom with floor-to-ceiling windows providing a panoramic view of Lake Michigan. As impressed as I'd been with the view from his main floor balcony, from this elevation the lake seemed to stretch out in every direction forever. But the view on the *inside* was even more spectacular. Bannon's bedroom was almost as large as most people's houses, with giant expressionist paintings hanging on the walls, a huge wood-burning fireplace next to the bed, and a separate bar beside the sliding glass windows.

"Would you like something to drink?" he said, lifting a crystal decanter off the table. "Perhaps a glass of brandy? I've got a thirty-year-old bottle of Hennessey that I've been meaning to open for a special event."

As much as I admired his impressive collection of personal effects, I was far more attracted to the elaborate trimmings of his beautiful wife.

"That would be lovely," I said, smiling at Genevieve.

Bannon handed each of us a large goblet filled with cognac, then he pressed a remote control device and the large window panes began to separate, bringing in a gust of cool air.

"Would you like to move to the balcony? The view is even more magical at this time of the night."

"Sure," I said, checking with Hannah to make sure she was still feeling comfortable. She simply peered back at me with wide eyes and nodded silently. We stepped out onto the deck and Bannon motioned to a wicker settee encircling a bubbling Jacuzzi.

"It might be a bit warmer next to the hot tub," he said, extending his hand toward the tub. "Please—make yourselves comfortable."

Hannan and I took a spot next to one another, while Bannon and his wife sat kitty-corner to us, a few feet to our left. The view of the lake was magnificent with the light of the full moon reflecting off the ripples like an evening sunset on a secluded beach. A cool breeze wafted in from the shore, and I pulled my vest over my exposed abdomen.

"Feel free to dip your toes in the water," he said. "Or climb right in if you prefer. It's chillier outside than usual tonight."

"I wouldn't mind getting out of these boots," I said, kicking off my footwear and placing my feet in the churning water.

Then I turned to Hannah and smiled.

"This feels heavenly, Han. Why don't you join me?"

She motioned to her all-in-one ensemble and frowned.

"It's not quite as simple for me as it is for you."

"Don't be concerned about *us*," Bannon grinned. "We're all adults here. Besides, I think we've seen just about everything already tonight. No one's watching this time besides Genevieve and me."

Hannah peered at me for a moment and I nodded. I'd never known her to be shy in these kinds of circumstances and it didn't take long for her to shed her clothes and slide under the bubbling water.

"Mmm," she purred, glancing up at me. "It's lovely. You should come in. These jets are good for massaging more than just your feet."

I looked toward Bannon and his wife and they smiled with a knowing grin.

"You said you wanted to find a private spot to continue your engagement," he said. "Don't let us stop you. We'll just finish our brandies while you two make yourselves comfortable."

He glanced down at my bobbing tool then peered back up at me.

"Is your equipment waterproof?"

"It should be," I said, winking toward Hannah. "Would you like me to keep it on?"

"I think we would," Bannon grinned. "I'd love to see how you use that thing close-up. How about you, dear? Are you interested in watching Jade play with her magic wand again?"

"Absolutely," Genevieve said, staring me directly in the eye. "I'd love to see her make another pretty girl come with her big man-cock."

I pulled off my chaps and vest and squeezed the trigger on my pistol to re-inflate my shaft to its full length then pressed the button on the handle to turn on the vibrator. Bannon and Genevieve squinted at the humming device, and I smiled at them as I slipped under the surface next to Hannah.

She scooted up next to me and lowered her hand under the water, stroking my phallus as she caressed the inside of my thighs. I turned toward her and we embraced in a passionate kiss. I could feel the jets of the Jacuzzi shooting between our breasts as we rubbed our tits together while she lifted her leg, straddling my hips. Within seconds, she lowered herself onto my pole and wrapped her arms around my back. As she began to rock her hips together with mine, I glanced up and made eye contact with Bannon and his wife. I noticed the front of his toga was tenting between his legs and Genevieve's hand was moving up and down as he smiled lasciviously toward us.

"Damn, Jade," Hannah groaned as I embedded my rod deep inside her. "That thing feels amazing. Fuck me with your big cock. Rub your balls on my cunt. I can feel it vibrating."

"Mmm," I sighed, as her tits mashed up against mine in the swirling water. "Squeeze my dick, Hannah. Let's put on a nice show for our hosts."

By now, Bannon had dispensed with any form of modesty, flinging his toga to the side where I could see his throbbing erection standing up between his spread legs. Judging by the size of his wife's hand, he appeared to have a decent-sized hard-on, but nowhere near as large as my own. Genevieve had apparently gotten just worked up watching Hannah and me fucking under the swirling water, and before long she kicked off her heels and hiked up her dress, sitting down over her husband's cock while she faced us. As I darted my eyes between her husband's prick thrusting in and out of her pussy and her dark eyes, our mouths began to open in mutual pleasure.

It was an incredible turn-on watching Genevieve's sexy body squirming over her husband's cock as she watched the two of us writhing in the churning water. Whether she was more excited getting fucked by her husband while two pretty girls watched them get it on or by the sight of Hannan and me enjoying ourselves underneath the surface, it didn't matter. Before long, all four of us were moaning loudly as we watched each other fuck our partners with abandon.

Hannah was the first to go off, as she started shaking wildly on my hips.

"Oh God, Jade," she groaned. "I'm cumming! Ram it inside me. Let me feel your balls slap up against me. Uhnnnnnn!"

Seeing Hannah having a powerful orgasm on top of me soon put Bannon over the edge as he grunted with his shaft pulsing inside his wife's pussy. Although he was staring at me, I was more interested in watching the expression on Genevieve's face as she returned my gaze with glassy eyes. I could tell that she was close, but needed a little extra stimulation to reach her goal.

As she locked eyes on me, she placed her hand over the front of her mound and began jerking her protruding nub. As her eyes opened progressively wider, I leaned forward and lifted my ass over one of the jets behind me. While the water gushed against my quivering opening, the vibrating balls pressed against my clit, and I felt a surge of pleasure engulfing my body.

"I'm close," I panted, locking eyes with Bannon's wife. "Come for me, Genevieve. Let me watch you come all over my big dick."

Even though she was planted on her husband's cock, we were both thinking the same thing. In that moment of mutual ecstasy, we were both imagining that it was *my* cock embedded in her pussy instead of her husband's.

"Yes, Jade!" she howled. "I'm cumming! I feel you inside me. I want you so bad. Oh *Gawd*..."

While the four of us panted and groaned in simultaneous climax, I glanced at Bannon, noticing him watching me with a wild look in his eye. Locked on me with laser focus, he had a strange, almost animalistic expression. I wasn't sure what he was channeling at that moment, but I could tell it wasn't his wife he was thinking about.

After we all settled down, Genevieve lifted herself off her husband's cock and slid in the water next to Hannah and me. She cuddled up beside me and her hand disappeared under the water, and soon after I felt her caressing my vibrating dildo. As Hannah leaned over to kiss her, Bannon stood up with his penis dripping a string of cum, motioning with his head inside his bed chamber.

"Why don't we all go back inside?" he said. "There'll be more room for us to play and we can watch each other better on the bed. Something tells me there's still a lot of pent-up energy between you girls."

Genevieve stepped up out of the tub first and led me by the hand into the bedroom as Hannah scampered in behind us, shivering. Bannon returned from his washroom and threw each of us a towel. Then he walked over to the bed and sat on the edge, beckoning for the rest of us to join him.

"Come," he said. "Let's share the wealth. There's plenty to go around."

"What did you have in mind?" I said, raising my eyebrows. After the Tarzan episode, I wasn't sure what part of me he was more interested in.

"There's enough parts between us for us to create an interesting *foursome*, don't you think?" he smirked.

As we all lay down on the bed and began exploring each other's bodies, Bannon seemed immediately drawn to my cock. As he sucked on my nipples, he reached down and began stroking my phallus while he masturbated himself with his other hand. While Hannah and Jenny intertwined their legs and began rubbing their pussies together, Bannon lowered himself down my abdomen until his face was directly in front of my giant pole. Suddenly, he stretched his lips around the head and began sucking it while he jerked his hand over his own dripping dick. Within seconds, he began moaning loudly, as he jetted squirts of cum all over his stomach.

Seeing her husband getting off so quickly again, Genevieve sat up and peered at the two of us with a sly smile.

"You seem quite enamored with Jade's cock, dear. I have an idea, if you're game for a little four-way fun. How would you like a *real* cock inside you this time, Hannah?"

Hannah looked at Genevieve then back at her husband, and smiled. There was little doubt that she'd fantasized about being fucked by the hot billionaire for a long time.

"*Definitely*," she said.

"Lie down face up on the bed," Genevieve instructed. "That way we can *both* have access to you. And *Jade*," she purred, with a gleam in her eye. "Why don't you choose whatever outlet looks most enticing to you among the three of us?"

As Genevieve spread her thighs over Hannah's face and lowered her pussy onto her lips, Bannon pulled Hannah's legs apart and straddled her opening with his dripping dick. As I watched them begin to fuck my best friend like she was a piece of meat, something inside me snapped. There was something about the way Bannon thought he could use her any way he wanted that pissed me off.

Just another self-righteous rich asshole, I thought. *This guy needs to be put in his place.*

As I kneeled behind him watching the two of them grinding their bodies against Hannah, Genevieve looked up at me and smiled. She glanced down toward her husband's ass and nodded. It was almost like she was *begging* me to fuck him from behind.

As the sides of my lips slowly curled up in acknowledgement, I brushed my erect dildo over Bannon's cheeks. Instead of flinching, he leaned further forward until I could see his balls waggling above Hannah's pussy. His asshole puckered as he thrust in and out of her, and for the first time in my life, I sensed the attraction of anal sex. There was something incredibly sexy and empowering about fucking a man up the ass. Now I knew why gay men separated into tops and bottoms. Just as with lesbian couples, one had to be the dominant one and one was meant to be the submissive one.

And *this* time, it was *my* turn to be the dominant one. Only in a way I'd never envisioned.

I lifted the tip of my pole, still glistening with Hannah's juices, and pointed it toward Bannon's opening. As I pressed it against his pucker, he grunted and pushed back gently.

So he likes being fucked by a woman? I thought. *It's time to show him who's really in charge here.*

I grabbed the sides of his hips and slowly pressed my cock deeper inside him. It felt strange and titillating at the same time to be fucking a man with my faux hard-on. As my balls pressed back against my clit, I imagined what it would feel like for a man to fuck another man this way. Suddenly, all the times I'd felt used by men who fucked from behind came flooding back. I thrust my dick as far into Bannon's ass as I could and began pounding my hips against his butt cheeks.

As his hole stretched as far as it could go by my coke-can-width hard-on, I found myself enjoying the feeling of thrusting in and out of him. Strangely, Genevieve seemed to be enjoying the show almost as much as me, as she writhed and moaned on Hannah's face while watching the two of us.

"Yes, Jade," she grunted. "Fuck Jack's ass. Make him your bitch. I want to watch him get off while you have your way with him."

Whether it was the sight of her pretty body twisting over Hannah's face or the sense of power I felt fucking her husband, I soon felt the familiar wall of pleasure beginning to overtake me. As I pressed my balls tight against his ass, creating more friction against my clit, I began to moan approaching my peak.

"Damn this is hot," I grunted. "I'm going to come soon. Watch me cum inside your husband's ass, Genevieve."

"Yes," she groaned, suddenly shifting her gaze to her husband's eyes.

I wasn't sure if she was communing with him at that moment or she just enjoyed seeing him at his most vulnerable moment. Either way, the sight of her convulsing over Hannah's mouth as she reached her own orgasm soon opened my floodgates. I pulled Bannon's ass hard toward me as I thrust my cock one last time deep into him, squirting all over my vibrating balls and Hannah's pussy. Within seconds, all four of us were howling in mutual ecstasy as we pounded and quivered atop one another in a mass of sweaty flesh. When we finally collapsed onto the bed in exhaustion, Genevieve leaned over and kissed me, whispering in my ear.

"Thanks for putting my husband in his rightful place," she mewed. "You have no idea how much both of us needed that."

VOLUME FIVE

THE MASSEUSE

1

———————

Ever since my playdate with Hannah at the rooftop spa in downtown Chicago, I felt a certain void in my love life. I'd enjoyed the various flings with my many lovers over the past few months, but there was always an expectation when the sex was over to move on to the next stage of intimacy. If either partner wasn't ready to invest further in the relationship, inevitably someone's feelings got hurt when one or the other walked away. Every now and then, it was nice to just have a simple, no-strings-attached, take-no-prisoners *hook-up*.

But it was more than that. I longed for the experience of being *feted*, of having my body worshipped by someone whose only focus was giving me the maximum amount of pleasure in the limited amount of time we were together. I wanted to return full-circle to my first experimental foray into the world of anonymous sex at the Fantasy Feast dinner party where I could lie back and let someone service my body. Even if I had to pay for it.

One lonely night when I needed to feel the touch of someone's else's hands on my body, I flipped open my laptop and typed in the search words *private masseuse*. I knew it had to be a female, not a man. Beyond my rapidly increasing proclivity toward having sex only with other women, the kind of massage I had in mind involved more than just the typical therapeutic rub-down. When things got hot and heavy, I needed my partner to keep his dick in his pants while focusing his attention only on pleasing me.

Which was something I'd found very few men capable of doing.

The first few results that came up on the screen provided a list of 'licensed massage therapists' who were available to make house calls in my area. But I knew this was code for the traditional, non-sexual type of massage. Besides, I wasn't sure I wanted my new paramour to know where I lived. Beyond the prying eyes of my nosy neighbors, I didn't want to experience another awkward moment when I had to kick another putative lover out of my house. I wanted to walk in, an out, freely on my own terms from this professional relationship.

I scrolled a little further down the page and hesitated when I saw a listing titled *White Orchid Massage–experience the pleasure of tantric massage.*

Okay, I thought. This sounds a little bit more like what I'm looking for. The word 'tantric' suggested a slightly *different* kind of massage treatment.

I clicked on the link and a description appeared beside a picture of a scantily clad masseuse massaging a woman's bare lower back:

Tantric massage is the art of caressing one's body where the boundaries disappear and the recipient learns to experience an elevated and prolonged form of pleasure and relaxation. Your energy flow is stimulated by our personal Goddesses while your senses are gradually awakened toward their maximum potential. Particular attention is focused on attending to the sensitive personal areas of a man's lingam or a woman's yoni. Book a session today to experience the ultimate expression of personal body worship.

Yes, I thought. *That's what I'm talking about: personal body worship. This is what I've been looking for. But who exactly are these goddesses, and what do they mean by a man's lingam and a woman's yoni?*

I clicked on the button below marked *Lingam Massage,* and some black and white illustrations of a woman's hands massaging a man's erect penis appeared with a text box to the side.

> *The Sanskrit word for the male sex organ is Lingam, which is loosely translated as the 'Wand of Light'. In tantra, the Lingam is honored as the vessel that channels a man's creative energy and pleasure. The goal of the one-hour lingam massage is to caress the entire sensitive area including the testicles, perineum, and the Sacred Spot (prostate), allowing the man to surrender to a new, enlightened form of pleasure. Orgasm is not necessarily the goal, but it can be a welcome and pleasant side effect.*

Orgasm isn't the goal? What the hell else do you expect the recipient to experience after one hour of massaging his dick, balls, and perineum?

But I liked the symbolism behind the words 'honoring' his sexual organ and enabling him to experience an 'enlightened form of pleasure'. Something told me that although orgasm wasn't the primary goal, most clients of this special form of massage therapy left with a very happy ending.

But it wasn't *male* pleasure and orgasm that I was interested in. I wanted these special massage goddesses to focus on administering a unique form of female-oriented pleasure. I clicked on the next button marked *Yoni Massage*, and some more erotic illustrations of a woman's hands massaging a woman's vulva appeared with another line of text below.

> *Yoni is the Sanskrit word for the vagina, which means the 'sacred temple' of a woman's body. During the yoni massage, the Goddess creates a unique space for the receiver to relax, from which she can enter a heightened state of arousal and ultimate pleasure. When orgasm does occur, it is often more expanded and more satisfying. While delivering a yoni massage, the giver should not expect anything in return, but simply allow the receiver to enjoy the experience and lose herself in the prolonged pleasure of being worshipped for the sexual person she is.*

Fuck yes, I panted out loud. That's exactly what I wanted.

Someone to focus her attention entirely on my pleasure, who'd tease and torment me until I experienced the ultimate form of satisfaction. But even though I knew it would be an entirely one-way form of erotic stimulation, I still needed to be able to connect in some way with my partner. What did these so-called Goddesses look like? I wouldn't be able to truly immerse myself in the experience if I didn't find her attractive.

My gaze shifted to the menu on the sidebar, where a map displayed red pins showing the location of White Orchid goddesses in major cities throughout the United States. I clicked on the pin centered over Chicago and a photo of a pretty African-American girl named Violet appeared with a link for more details. The page opened with a picture of a dark, slender woman about my age wearing a skimpy leotard that hugged every inch of her lithe figure. It showed her leaning over a massage table while caressing the upper thighs of another woman lying face down with a small towel barely covering her upturned ass.

But it was *Violet's* ass that drew my immediate attention. Slender and curvy with separate volleyball-sized globes, the downward seam of her tights divided them into perfectly shaped spheres that made it look like her butt had been carved out of marble. I felt my panties begin to dampen as I imagined watching her sylphlike figure flexing and bending while she laid her hands on my body. I read the brief bio beside her picture, then my attention was drawn to the top of the page where a drop-down menu outlined her list of services.

I clicked on the Yoni Massage button, where some erotic pictures of Georgia O'Keefe floral artwork framed the detailed description of her ninety-minute intimate massage sessions. Although the verbiage referred to cryptic terms such as 'somatic pelvic floor exercises' and 'sexual energy cultivation techniques', I had little doubt, just as with the thinly-veiled symbolism of the Georgia O'Keefe paintings, where exactly she intended to focus her attention.

The massage sessions were provided at her personal studio and offered in blocks of four, each lasting roughly ninety minutes, with home assignments and email check-ins between sessions. There was no appointment form or payment link–only an email address where I was encouraged to leave a detailed message with my personal details and booking requests. I immediately clicked on the link and began composing a carefully worded message:

Violet,

I'm interested in booking a session for your one-on-one personal yoni massage. I work from home, so I'm available pretty much any time to meet at your studio, but weekends are my preferred time to concentrate on personal enrichment.

Please let me know the next available slot you have to fit me in. I look forward to learning more about your tantric exercises and experiencing your enlightened form of body worship.

Sincerely,

Jade

After I clicked send, I immediately winced at my not-so-subtle choice of words asking for a 'slot' to fit me in. But as I continued scanning her website page further describing the yoni massage procedure accompanied with more illustrations of the masseuse probing her client's orifices in various sexy positions, I pulled down my panties and thrust my fingers inside my hole, mimicking the Goddess's techniques.

You can press your fingers into my slot any way you like, I panted, running my eyes over her tight figure while I hunched over my keyboard feeling my pleasure beginning to rise...

2

———————

By the time I finished coming down from my self-induced orgasm, I already had a new message notification in my inbox. I opened my mail and excitedly clicked on the message from GoddessViolet.

Jade,

Thank you for your inquiry regarding my services. I have an opening for yoni massage this Sunday at 2 p.m. if that works for you.

My fees are $600 for a four-massage package, with each massage offering a deeper and more intense stimulation of your sacred temple. I also offer a separate introductory massage for $200.

Please click on the PayPal link below to select and make advance payment for your preferred option. Once you complete the payment, I'll send another email with the address for my studio.

I look forward to our time together and feel blessed to share these transformative practices with you.

Love and blessings,

Violet

After reading her message, I sat back in my chair, contemplating my options. Six hundred bucks was a considerable sum, and although everything looked above-board on her website, I still couldn't be sure this wasn't some kind of scam. I clicked on the payment link and chose the two hundred dollar introductory option, then waited patiently for a reply with the additional details. It took a painfully long time for her to reply, but after she confirmed receipt of my payment and provided me with the location of her private studio, I breathed a sigh of relief.

For the next three days, I grew increasingly excited about my upcoming encounter, shaving my legs and armpits twice to make sure there'd be no unnecessary friction between any part of my skin and Violet's soft hands. Fortunately, my earlier laser hair treatment had already removed the last traces of any hairs from my mound and vulva. I must have come at least ten more times lying in front of my dressing room mirror imagining the sexy masseuse exploring every inch of my body.

By the time Sunday came around, my skin already felt like pins and needles in anticipation of Violet's tantric caresses. There was something about the idea of lying down and letting somebody bring me to the height of pleasure while she watched me writhe and moan in front of her that drove me crazy with desire. I'd always enjoyed having someone manually manipulate me to orgasm as much as oral or full-contact sex, knowing they could just sit back and savor my sexual response while concentrating all their energies on pleasing me.

When I drove to the address provided by Violet in her email, I was relieved to see it wasn't a cheap strip mall typical of those quick rub-and-tug operations. On the contrary, it was a beautiful luxury highrise with a commanding view of Lake Michigan only a few blocks away. If this was her primary source of income, I thought with a smile, she must run a pretty good book of business. I parked my car in the guest parking area then headed to the foyer where I buzzed the button for suite 2402.

"Hello?" a soft voice answered after a brief pause.

"It's Jade," I said. "I have a two p.m. appointment."

There was a loud buzz and I opened the unlocked entrance door then made my way to the elevator bank. I found it odd that she hadn't offered a more friendly greeting before buzzing me in, and during the long elevator ride to the twenty-fourth floor, I suddenly began to have second thoughts.

Just how safe is it to be walking into a stranger's highrise on the pretense of anonymous sex? I'd always wondered why most masseuses preferred to provide the service at their clients' homes rather than their own residence. Was this some kind of trap where someone just *pretending* to be Violet enticed me into his home only to hold me prisoner and have his way with me?

I was just about to tap out a warning message to my best friend Hannah on my phone when the elevator opened. The hallway was tastefully decorated with plush wool carpets, brightly illuminated wall sconces, and expensive brass door fixtures. I peered down the corridor in the direction of Violet's apartment near the end and put my phone back in my purse.

Fuck it, I said to myself, shaking the cobwebs out of my head. *If someone wanted to lure me into some kind of dangerous arrangement, they wouldn't do it in a place like this. Or give me their address, which I could easily share with my friends. She's probably doing this at her place as much to protect herself as me.*

When I reached her door, I paused to summon my courage, then tapped twice on the shiny lacquer surface.

Even the entrance to her 'studio' is upscale and enticing, I thought.

When the door swung open and I saw Violet peering out at me with a sweet smile, I breathed a sigh of relief. She was wearing a long silk kimono with a single white orchid nestled in the side of her upswept hair held back in a pretty bun. She was lighter-skinned than she appeared on the website, and with her smooth, caramel-colored complexion, large brown eyes and full sensuous lips, she reminded me of young Beyoncé.

"Good afternoon," she said standing to the side, motioning for me to enter her apartment.

When I walked through the door, she offered to take my coat then hung it in the adjacent closet. She led me to a large living room dominated by floor-to-ceiling windows displaying an unobstructed view of Lake Michigan, glistening like a sparkling jewel in the mid-afternoon sun. Her apartment was tastefully decorated in a minimal Japanese ethos, with a low-slung sectional sofa, large glass coffee table, and floral prints of George O'Keefe paintings on the wall. In the center of the room stood a long massage table covered in a white terrycloth towel.

My pussy fluttered at the sensual imagery of the setting and I peered at Violet with raised eyebrows.

"Wow," I said. "I've never had a massage in such a beautiful place. You have magnificent taste in your decor."

"Thank you," she said, motioning to a closed door a few feet behind her. "If you'd like to get changed, you can use my powder room. You'll find a cotton robe hanging on the back of the door."

"Thank you," I said, taking her cue to not waste any time and opening the door to the change room.

When I got inside, I closed it softly behind me, then leaned back against the partition while staring at myself in the oval mirror over the vanity.

Holy fuck! I mouthed the words silently, looking at myself in disbelief. Not only was Violet even more beautiful in person than she appeared on her website, her massage studio was something out of a fantasy dream. This wasn't some cheap massage parlor where you'd walk in for a quickie then hightail it out of there so as not to be seen. This was more like the luxury upscale spa Hannah and I'd gone to a few months earlier where we were feted and spoiled for much of the day. The difference was that in *this* place, I had both the masseuse *and* the exquisite surroundings all to myself for the next ninety minutes.

As I began disrobing and neatly folding my clothes on the tasteful sidestand to the left side of the sink, I began singing the melody to the Beyoncé song Irreplaceable.

To the left, to the left
To the left, to the left
Everything you own in the box to the left

In the closet that's my stuff, yes
If I bought it please don't touch...

I'd always thought the singer was one of the most beautiful women I'd ever seen. I must have watched the sexy video of that song a hundred times, fantasizing that it was me squatting over her sexy legs while she sat in front of her makeup mirror in a slinky negligee. And now I had the chance to relive my fantasy with a dead ringer who was about to touch me in the most intimate way.

After I removed all my clothes, I looked at myself in the mirror appraising my naked, freshly primped body. I still had a pretty sexy figure for a woman in her mid-thirties, with firm plump breasts sitting high on my chest, a narrow, toned waist, and long slender legs. I wondered how much attention the *front* of my body would get from Violet during this first encounter. I knew most masseuses only attended to the back of their clients' bodies while focusing on relaxing and removing the knots from their muscles, rather than stimulating the more erogenous areas of their figures.

No matter, I said to myself, slipping my arms through the sleeves of the waffle-patterned robe hanging on the back of the door and tying the belt loosely around my waist before swinging the door open.

Either way, I planned to give my sexy masseuse ample access to my 'sacred places', whether I was lying face down or face up.

3

———————

When I emerged from the powder room, I was surprised to see that Violet had removed her robe and was preparing her tools on a side table next to the massage table. Instead of the long silk robe, she was now wearing a thin cotton tank top with matching white cotton tights. The tight fabric clung to every curvature of her body and when she swung around to greet me, I gasped audibly when I saw her full figure for the first time.

Her breasts were petite, but they had an exquisite elongated, scooped shape that made the front of her skimpy t-shirt tent and bulge with prominent sensuous darts poking out from her hardened nipples. Her thin cotton tights also left a minimal amount to the imagination, with the soft fabric flowing over her flat pelvis and sensuously curved hips to her shapely, well-toned legs. I could see the cleft from the slit of her pussy as the fabric clung to her like a second skin, daring me to soak up her body with my wide eyes. In a way, it was even *more* erotic to see her cloaked in the soft white covering barely concealing her dark areolas and sexy camel toe, beckoning for me to approach her closer.

"May I take your robe?" she said, holding out her Madonna-toned arms in front of her.

"Um–yes," I stammered, momentarily pulled out of my trance.

I turned around and she softly pulled the robe off my shoulders then placed it on a side table beside the sofa. I peered at the massage table inquisitively, then turned back around to face Violet.

"Do you want me to lie face up or down?" I said, unsure of the protocol with this new procedure.

"Let's go face down to start," she smiled, extending her arm toward the table.

I lifted my right knee and climbed onto the bench, extending my legs straight down behind me. There was no customary hole at the head of the table where I'd normally place my face to relax my neck muscles, so I turned my head to peer out over the wide expanse of sparkling blue water. As soon as I saw the soothing picture of the gently lapping waves and reflected sunshine, I immediately began to feel the sexual tension ebb away. Whether this was by design or incidental, I wasn't sure. But for a few brief moments, I forgot about the primary purpose for my visit and flitted my eyelids in sublime bliss. Even if I just had to lie here watching this spectacular scenery for an hour and a half, it would almost be worth the two hundred dollar price of admission.

But it didn't take long for my *other* senses to be awakened as Violet opened her scented bottles of massage oil and the smell of jasmine and chamomile filled my nostrils. I breathed the heavenly scent in as I expanded my lungs and my chest rose and fell gently on the padded table. I could hear the sound of oil dribbling into her hands as she turned one of the bottles upside-down, then rubbed them together slowly. My pussy quivered knowing that she would soon lay her moistened hands on my skin, and I extended my arms to my side, inviting her to begin touching me.

I was a little disappointed when she started at the foot of the table with my feet, but I smiled peering up at the large analog clock hanging on the near wall, knowing she had a full ninety minutes to explore the rest of my body. I relaxed the muscles tensing in my shoulders and buttocks, happy to bide my time while she worked her way up toward my waiting temple.

As she separated each of my toes between her slippery fingers and kneaded them softly and sensuously, I was tempted to talk to her to break the awkward silence. But I knew from previous massages that masseuses preferred to work in silence, encouraging their clients to relax and let all the external distractions melt away. The whole point of a massage was to concentrate on the soothing feeling of being caressed, and I had no intention of disrupting Violet's mojo at the outset of our erotic encounter.

But that didn't stop me from letting my mind wander to all manner of sexual imagery while she squeezed and kneaded my extremities. As she pulled her fingers slowly down each of my toes from the ball of my foot to the toenails, I imagined it was my *clit* she was pinching between her fingers while she stroked my hard shaft and teased the tip of my nub. Whenever she slipped her fingers between my toes, I channeled her inserting her slender digits between my dripping *labia*, feeling my wet tunnel gripping her tightly. And when she grabbed my feet and pressed her thumbs against my soles while she pulled my toes against her washboard-hard tummy, I imagined toe-fucking her pussy while she gripped me in the throes of passion.

By the time her fingers moved to my ankles and began working their way up the inside of my calves, I was already soaking wet while I unconsciously ground my mound into the moistening towel beneath me. I spread my legs apart, inviting Violet to move closer to my apex, but she seemed in no hurry to attend to my quivering pussy. Instead, she wrapped her fingers around the curvature of my calves, rubbing them softly and slowly with her warm, slippery hands. Unlike the firm and sometimes painful kneading of my muscles that most masseurs were accustomed to administering, her touch was always light and sensuous, focused instead on titillating and stimulating every square inch of my skin. Reflecting back on what I'd read on the White Orchid website, I knew that she had a plan for eventually reaching my 'sacred temple', with the goal of heightening my arousal to achieve the 'ultimate pleasure'.

I tried to relax my arms and the rest of my body while she worked her way further up the inside of my thighs, but I couldn't help curling my upturned fingers in a come-hither motion in the direction of my aching sex. But just as her thumbs began probing the edges of my tumescent lips, she suddenly shifted position and moved up to the *head* of the table, placing her moist hands on my shoulders and upper back. This time I could detect the scent of my own juices intermingled with the aromatic massage oil as her hands slid over my pliant skin, and I turned my head away from the direction of the lake to watch Violet more closely.

As she stood to the side of the long table to gain better access to my upper back, I stared at her crotch while she leaned and stroked my shoulders and neck softly. The fabric of the white cotton tights pulled and stretched as she swayed her body overtop of me, and I could feel my mouth beginning to water while I imagined sucking her sweet pussy into my mouth. She must have known what was on my mind while she did this, because she hesitated for the longest time pressing the bottom of her undergarments sensuously against the padded corner of the table while she moved her hands progressively further down my back.

I was disappointed when she shifted position once again, denying me ready viewing access to her lower body, but I smiled when I noticed a small wet spot forming in the seam of her pants below her vulva. This time, she moved her hips directly over the top of my head while she extended her arms further down the center of my back toward my flexing buttocks. She placed her thumbs together, sliding them sensuously down the valley in the center of my back, and I lifted my ass, trying to narrow the distance between her probing fingers and my puckering lips. Making my torment all the more intense, while she pressed her palms further down my back in a series of forward-and-back movements, she gently pushed her pubis against the back of my head.

Whether she was doing this for her own amusement or mine, I couldn't be sure. But it took every ounce of my willpower not to lift my head and clamp onto her pussy like a wild boar catching its prey after a long chase through the underbrush. By now I was panting heavily, and she must have felt my breath on her upper thighs strad-dling either side of my head. As she neared the small of my back with her probing thumbs, I tilted my hips as far as I could in her direction, pointing the cleft of my ass directly up toward her face. The further she probed down my body, the closer her torso leaned over the surface of my back, until I could feel her pointy breasts and hard nipples touching my skin.

I groaned quietly, begging her to press her fingers into my crack. When she finally did, my cheeks quivered, anticipating her reaching my aching sex. Instead, she wrapped her hands around the globes of my ass and squeezed them firmly, tantalizing me with the tips of her fingers as they touched the outside edges of my external labia. I grunted more loudly and swiveled my butt in circles, signaling to her that I was desperate for her to administer to my yoni as her website had promised.

Recognizing my impatience, Violet released the pressure on my buttocks and threaded her thumbs into my crevasse, rolling them softly over my puckering rosebud. I groaned like a cat in heat when I felt her touch my sensitive tissue, and I spread my legs further apart to make it easier for her to slide her fingers over my crescent toward my swollen lips and buzzing clit. As she leaned her torso more firmly atop my back and pressed her mound harder against my moistening head, she began angling her palms inward, caressing the outside of my dripping labia with the tips of her fingers while she continued stimulating my sphincter with her thumbs. The combined sensation of her fingers probing my anus and the edges of my widening gash simultaneously was driving me crazy with passion, but she still hadn't touched me in the most sensitive area that would lead me toward a much-needed orgasm.

When she finally began pressing her fingers further down my crease toward my flaring slit and pinching my folds between her index and middle finger, sliding them sensuously along the length of my engorged labia, I hummed a sigh of pleasure knowing it wouldn't be long before Violet finally brought me to sexual nirvana. But just as she began pressing her digits into my pulsing hole, I heard a soft chime and she withdrew her hands from my private areas as quickly as she had entered.

I twisted my head to peer up at her inquisitively, and she turned around to face the large clock on the wall while reaching over to the side table to dry off her dripping hands with a small towel. I looked up at the clock and was horrified to see the large hand pointing straight down, marking the completion of our session at three-thirty. Somehow, in all the heat of the slow buildup, I'd completely lost track of time.

"It appears that our time's up for today," Violet said nonchalantly. "I hope you enjoyed your introduction to tantric massage."

So that's her game, I thought, shaking my head in dismay. *She suckers me in with this so-called introductory session, driving me to the point of near-delirium then sends me packing just as I'm about to get off. Talk about a honey trap.*

I was pissed beyond belief, but the sight of Violet standing before me with the front of her cotton ensemble drenched in a combination of massage oil and my own sensual juices soon made me forget about her questionable business practice. The wetness had made her t-shirt nearly transparent, and I gawked like a newborn baby at her large brown medallions and pointed nipples pressing against the thin fabric. Even the front of her *tights* was soaking wet, pulled up between her flaring labia at the base of her mound. I wasn't sure if it was from her own juices released while she was grinding against my head or from the sweat pouring out of my hair as I got increasingly turned on, but it didn't matter. All I could think about was continuing her program of tantric massage and getting as close as I could to this beautiful goddess again as soon as possible. She had me hooked like a fish, and she knew it.

"How soon are you available for another session?" I asked meekly, sitting up on top of the giant wet spot I'd created in the middle of the massage table.

4

———

After my equally titillating and frustrating initial massage session with Violet, I had to wait a whole week to see her again. In the intervening time, I vacillated between fuming over the disappointing ending she'd delivered and reliving her slow but intense buildup. Even though I didn't experience my usual climactic finish, I hadn't felt so turned on for so long in a very long time.

During my subsequent masturbation sessions, instead of rushing toward orgasm in the usual manner, I brought myself close to the edge repeatedly, resisting the temptation to fall over the precipice and quickly come down from my highs. There was something strangely liberating about being able to sustain such intense pleasure for as long as I wanted without always feeling the need for the final payoff. If this was what tantric sex was all about, I was rapidly becoming a passionate proponent of the mysterious practice.

By the time the following Sunday rolled around, my entire body was buzzing from my extended edging sessions, and I was eager to feel Violet's magic hands upon me once again. When I arrived at her studio and she opened the door, she was already wearing her sensuous white cotton undergarments, and we wasted no time getting started.

"Face up or face down?" I asked succinctly after shedding my street clothes in her powder room.

"Down," she said, equally matter-of-factly.

I climbed up on the padded massage table and extended my arms behind me, turning my head to peer out at the calming expanse of blue water extending out to the horizon. This time I was determined to relax and simply enjoy the voyage Violet took me on, realizing this process was far more about the journey than the destination.

She began once again at the foot of my body, but this time, instead of clasping both of my feet at the same time, she focused her attention only on my left foot, caressing the hard instep and my soft sole with gentle circular motions of her moistened hands. I could smell the gentle aroma of apple intermingled with the other scented oils, and my mouth began to water once again imagining myself lapping up her juices as she approached my erogenous zones. The combination of her firm kneading of my dorsal bone and the soft pressing of her digits into the pliant flesh of my sole reminded me of the sensation of a lover running her hands down over my pubis into the loose folds of my vulva. I purred like a kitten soaking up the exquisite slowness and eroticism of her touch.

As she shifted toward the top of my foot, instead of moving up the insides of my lower legs, this time she rolled her hands over the bump on the outside of my ankle like a pitcher softening up a base-ball before delivering it to the opposing batter. Except in this case, I was transfixed by her pre-delivery ritual, already losing focus on why I was hunched over the plate, watching her graceful movement in the reflection of the big picture window.

When she began running her hands up along the outside edge of my leg, I couldn't help flexing my calves and thighs in autonomic response to her sensuous touch. As she approached my downturned pelvis, she slipped her fingers under my hips, tracing the curved ridge along the top of my crest. Although her fingers never got closer than a few inches from my tingling mound and pussy, the feeling of her sliding her fingers over my hard bone was one of the most erotic sensations I'd ever experienced.

I tilted my body a few inches away from her to give her some more space, and she pushed me further onto my side, with the front of my body now facing her. I turned my face to peer in her direction and was happy to see her newly oil-stained bodysuit displaying her beautiful brown skin underneath.

As she began running her palms over the side indentation of my waist, I could feel the goose bumps on my skin beginning to rise while I watched her tits jiggling in her tight tank-top. Although the upper part of her ensemble wasn't as wet as the lower portion, I could see her large brown areolas and protruding peaks through the light-colored fabric, daring me not to ogle them like a star-struck fangirl.

When she placed her palms on my quivering tummy and began moving her hands toward my mashed-together breasts, my mouth opened unconsciously, desperately wanting to suck on her succulent teats. I could feel my own tips hardening the closer she got to my mounds, and when she encircled them with her palms, rolling the tips between her thumbs and forefingers, I gasped at how delicious it felt. I'd heard rumors how some women unconsciously reached orgasm from breast-feeding their babies, and now I understood how sensitive this part of the body could get when properly stimulated and caressed.

I groaned as Violet cupped my breasts, teasing me ever-so-gently with her warm, oily hands and soft fingertips. I probably could have come if she'd continued twisting and rolling my nubs for much longer, but just as before, she moved on just as I was nearing the turning point. I was sad to see her take her attention away from my engorged tits, but what she did next soon had me wishing she'd climb on top of me and have done with me.

Tilting my upper body further back, she pressed her palms firmly against my upper chest while she spread her fingers apart approaching my neck. As she encircled my narrow isthmus, I tilted my head up, and she squeezed my throat gently with the open palms of her hands. I'd never felt so vulnerable and sexually charged having someone else's hands on me, and I grunted like a wild animal lost in the clutches of a predator. While she was doing this, I could have sworn that her nipples pressed even further out against the flimsy fabric of her cotton t-shirt, and I detected a slight upward curl of her lips as she grasped me in the delicate embrace.

Was she getting just as turned on as I was from all this sexy imagery?

If so, I was more than happy for her to take whatever further advantage she desired of me, feeling my body's sexual energy rapidly rounding second base. But she obviously had no intention of suffocating me, and her hands continued their upward momentum as they rolled over my chin and jawline. When her apple-scented fingers moved next to my lips, I opened my mouth and she curled them into my cavity while I sucked on the tasty juices and kneaded her phalanges playfully with the tips of my teeth.

Two can play this game, I smiled, preventing her fingers from pulling out of me while I glared up at her with piercing eyes.

Instead of trying to remove her trapped fingers from my mouth, she curled her thumbs around the dripping edges of my lips, tracing a line around the raised edges, mimicking the caress of my outer labia. When I unconsciously groaned from the symbolism of her erotic touch, she pulled her fingers out from my loosened grip, then glided them up the side of my cheeks toward the bottom of my ears, curling them around their perimeter and pinching her fingers around the outside edges.

By now, I was moaning like a cat in heat and twisting my body in sexual abandon, eager for her to take me anyway she could. Her slow, teasing buildup was driving me crazy with desire, and I clasped the sides of her forearms, trying to pull her toward me. But she tensed the muscles in her strong arms as she resisted my attempt, running her oily fingers through my hair and over the back of my scalp. I didn't care for a millisecond that she was making a mess of my carefully coiffed hair while I looked up at her, begging her to fuck me.

Seeming to acknowledge my torment, she pulled her hands away from my face and moved them slowly across the side of my shoulder, tracing a line down the side of my arm with the lightest of touches, making my hairs stand up on end. When she reached my hand, she interlaced her fingers with mine, then lifted my arm, pressing it over my head. Then she clasped the underside of my upturned limb, threading her other hand with equal tenderness up the soft skin on the other side. When she reached my armpit, she paused for a moment, massaging the indented space firmly with her oily thumbs, now even further moistened from the saliva of my mouth.

"Oh God," I moaned, amazed at how her touching me in every place other than the most sensitive areas of my body could make me feel this electrified.

With my arm still held gently over the top of my head and lying pinned on my side, my breasts were pulled off-center and rolling atop one another, creating a new kind of sensation I hadn't felt before as my oiled flesh rubbed sensuously together. All the time I was moaning with every hair on my body standing on end, Violet watched me with her big doe eyes and glistening lips. I wanted desperately for her to lean over and suck my bullets into her mouth, bringing me to orgasm just like the breastfeeding mothers I'd heard about, but I knew that was too much to hope for at this still-early juncture.

She angled my arm gently back down onto my side, placing it softly on the table in front of me, then traced a line all the way down the hourglass-shaped side of my back, up and over the curvature of my ass and down the back of my upper thigh, pausing to caress the tender space behind the back of my knee. Then she pronated her hand and pulled my knee slowly up toward my hips, forcing my legs into a bent-knee scissor position.

I was now lying on my side on the massage table, drenched in massage oil, with my legs splayed into a side-split position, with the glistening gash of my billowy cunt freely displayed for her viewing pleasure. I could feel my juices pouring out of me while her gaze turned toward my slit, dripping over my engorged lips and down the front of my lower thigh. I felt incredibly sexy and exposed in this compromising position, and if she'd so much as *blown* anywhere in the direction of my flaring snatch, I'm sure I would have come in a nanosecond.

Realizing I was now about as aroused as I was ever going to be, Violet slowly rolled her palm over the arc of my upturned hip and turned her hand sideways, curving the side of it softly between the crack of my ass. The feeling of her oily hand slicing my cleft like a soft bread knife was another sensation I'd never felt before, and I tilted my pelvis toward her, desperately trying to bring her hand closer to my aching clit.

Clearly trying to extend my agony as long as possible, she waved the side of her hand gently up and down the length of my crease, stimulating my anus and the lower reaches of my opening with a slow, measured touch. Growing increasingly impatient, I glanced up at the wall and noticed that it was three-fifteen. There was only fifteen minutes left for Violet to bring me to the peak of pleasure. I was all for the idea of extending this intense feeling as long as possible, but sometimes a girl just needed to get off.

Noticing me peering up at the clock, Violet opened her hand and pressed her fingers further down toward my slit. When she reached my opening, I was elated when she curled them inside me, pressing her three middle fingers deep inside my tunnel. I groaned in excitement, angling my hips to extend them as far inside me as possible. For a few brief moments, I was content to simply hump her fingers embedded inside me, but the angle of her hand reaching over from the side made it difficult for her to stimulate my G-spot in the usual manner.

I twisted my hips in a circular motion trying to angle her hand in the direction of my most sensitive part and we she realized what I was attempting to do, she began flexing her index finger forward and back, finally caressing the magic spot on the inside of my pussy. I groaned in delight at the pleasant sensation, but something was still missing. As much as I was enjoying the feeling of her fingering my hole and teasing my G-spot, I still needed some direct contact with my clit.

I tilted my hips further upward, sliding her pinky up the outside edge of my labia and when I felt it make contact with my tingling gland, I groaned deeply, finally beginning to feel the familiar pangs of my orgasm approaching. Seeking to add more pleasure to my rapidly building excitement, Violet simultaneously extended her thumb toward my tight pucker as she circled her pinky over my swollen bulb.

Fuck yes, I thought, growling like a wildcat. Finally, she's hitting all the right buttons. I could feel my orgasm rapidly approaching, and I gripped the sides of the massage table while I stared at Violet's sexy tits pressing against the soft fabric of her t-shirt, preparing for the inevitable release. But just before I passed the moment of no return, the dreaded chime sounded again, and Violet paused with her hand deeply embedded in my tunnel. For a brief moment, I thought she was going to continue to finish me off, and I groaned when she began to pull her hand out of me.

What the fuck? I thought, panting wildly. *This isn't tantric massage— it's tantric torture! How can she do this to me, knowing how much I needed the ultimate release her website had clearly alluded to?* As she slowly began to clean up, I couldn't help asking the obvious question.

"That was wonderful," I said, sitting up reluctantly. "But when are you going to take me to that magical place of enlightenment your website promised?"

"Remember, the purpose of tantric massage isn't just about reaching sexual climax," she said, wiping the oil nonchalantly from her hands. "It's an opportunity for you to connect with your inner feelings and extend the pleasurable sensations to their maximum degree."

"But your website suggested that when orgasm is achieved this way, it is often more expanded and intense than usual. Isn't that one of the sensations you help your clients achieve at some point in this process?"

"Yes," she said. "But remember, you still have two more sessions in your scheduled package. Most of the pleasure is experienced during the slow and extended build-up."

"Okay," I said. "But I don't know if I'm going to be able to hold out much longer. What can I look forward to during my next session?"

"At stage three, the process will become more interactive, with closer contact between the two of us, adding an extra level of stimulation and excitement. I think you'll find the next stage in your journey takes you to an entirely new level of fulfilment."

I wasn't entirely sure what she meant by more *interactive*, but if it involved more body contact with her magnificent figure, I knew that would be more than enough to allow me to achieve my ultimate goal.

"You're a very demanding coach," I smiled. "I'm looking forward to improving my batting average the next time around."

"Next time we'll see if we can deliver some *home runs*," she nodded, adding to my athletic analogy.

R*eady for more erotic chills and thrills? Choose your next toe-curling fantasy from over thirty-five spicy stories in Jade's Erotic Adventures. Browse the full collection here:*

Click to scan your favorites...

FOLLOW VICTORIA RUSH:

Want to keep informed of my latest erotic book releases? Sign up for my newsletter and receive a FREE bonus book:

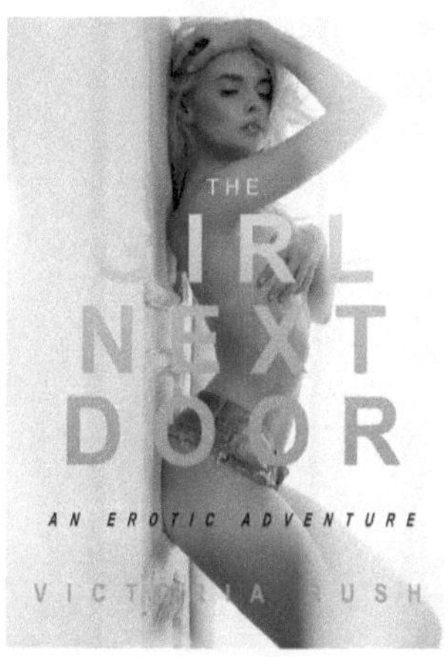

Spying on the neighbors just got a lot more interesting...